o illeraꝫ li mellor del mõ

fortiꝫ mal ꝓfaſaꝰ uoſ ꝼa

ꝺruiꝫ · Qⁱ uoſ confon ꝺꝛa

minar lieoinꝫ · per queſto

ueiſ aꝼꝛꝓ lauꝺiꝫ · Enoſ ena

pellon cꝛ nuiꝫ ·

Oſ uei que ꝺambaꝼ laſ paꝛꝫ

nemſ · Bauꝛaꝫ · per lauꝛen

gierꝫ beauꝫ · Anꝑꝰ eſenſ mã

tra non poſe lamer ꝺel foꝛ ·

Quen laſima enlaruiꝫ · vei

lauoleꝫa coꝛ ꝺuꝫ ·

Aꝛoꝛ eꝛaꝺreꝭ uan

iouenſ queſ ꝺᷓma uenaiꝫ ·

Lomaiꝫ el pluꝼ apenaꝫ aꝺ ꝗſ

graꝛuſ · Capel mueſꝛ truiol

A TROUBADOUR'S
TESTAMENT

A
TROUBADOUR'S
TESTAMENT

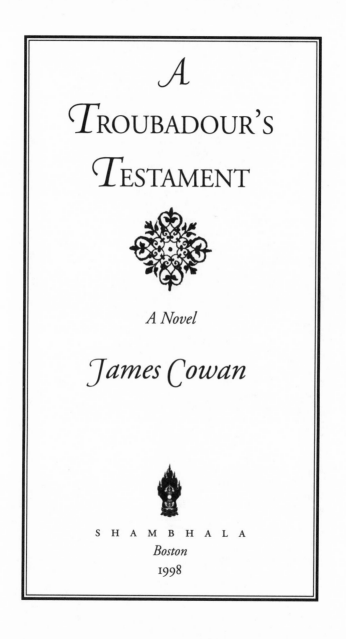

A Novel

James Cowan

SHAMBHALA

Boston

1998

The illustration reproduced on the endpapers is a detail
from a thirteenth-century illumninated manuscript written
by the historical Marcabrû. Reproduced by permission of the
Pierpont Morgan Library, New York (M.819, F269).

Shambhala Publications, Inc.
Horticultural Hall
300 Massachusetts Avenue
Boston, MA 02115
http://www.shambhala.com

9 8 7 6 5 4 3 2 1

First Edition

Printed in the United States of America

♾ This edition is printed on acid-free paper that meets the
American National Standards Institute Z39.48 Standard.

Distributed in the United States by Random House, Inc., and
in Canada by Random House of Canada Ltd

Library of Congress Cataloging-in-Publication Data

Cowan, James, 1942-

A Troubadour's Testament/by James Cowan.—1ST ed.
p. cm.
ISBN 1-57062-339-2 (cloth: acid-free paper)
I. Title.
PR9619.3.C597T7 1998   97-29650
823–dc21   CIP

For Wolfgang and Gabriela

I kept telling myself that to renounce the beautiful game of combining beautiful words was senseless, and that there was no reason to search for a single, and perhaps imaginary, word.

—JORGE LUIS BORGES

The reason for writing is to shelter something from death.

—ANDRÉ GIDE

CONTENTS

A TROUBADOUR'S
TESTAMENT

I

A PHONE CALL

After-dinner phone calls often convey grave tidings, but in this case I was in for a surprise. My friend R., who labored under a lifelong obsession with medieval architecture, called from his latest foray in southwestern France, this time to inform me that he had discovered something very unusual. In the tiny town of Ussel he had stumbled upon a *rouleau de mort,* a death roll, in the local museum, once the old Chapelle des Pénitents.

"A death roll?" I inquired, a little drowsy from the taste of a Bordeaux wine at table. "Does it belong to anyone I might know?"

"Of course. Your friend Marcebru. The twelfth-century poet you quote ad nauseam," R. added, put out by my casual air. "I uncovered it in a pile of papers in the museum."

I sat up in my chair. To find an unpublished manuscript belonging to the great troubadour poet Marcebru, some eight hundred years after his death, was indeed a coup. That the document came in the form of a death roll made the discovery all the more intriguing, since such rolls were more usually in the possession of wandering clerks or friars during the middle ages.

"What proof do you have that it belonged to him?" I asked, wary of it being a forgery. Being a specialist in French poetry, notably the works of François Villon, I was aware of the importance of such a discovery if it were true. As we possess fewer than forty of Marcebru's poems, any new discovery would greatly enhance our knowledge of this remarkable if irascible poet.

"The flavor, *mon vieux*. The taste of the verses that appear at the conclusion of the death roll. No one but Marcebru could create such lines as these," R. announced, hoping to dismiss my doubt. He then proceeded to recite over the phone a number of dark, bell-like verses in the Old Provençal tongue—verses I immediately recognized as those of Marcebru, so cogent were they, so austere was their resonance:

> *Per savi-l tenc ses doptanssa*
> *Cel qui de mon chant devina*

So que chascus motz declina,
Si cum la razos despleia,
Qu'ieu mezeis sui en erranssa
D'esclarzir parau l'escura.

The man who hears my song
And understands every word
As its theme unfolds, I consider
Indisputably wise, for I'm troubled
Myself by the task of making
Clear the obscurity of words.

"You have left me utterly speechless," I murmured.

"Poets have a way of doing this to us, don't you think?" R. replied, sensing the importance of his discovery. "You'd better get down here as soon as possible. I'm sure other researchers will rush to get a look at the death roll now that its presence is known. In any case, I believe its contents are explosive. It may ignite in your absence."

Then he rang off.

I had studied the lyrics of the medieval troubadours and had grown to respect their unsullied vision, the joy they had managed to bestow upon their age. They offered a gift in troubled times, when the voice of freedom was under threat from religious intolerance and social upheaval. People needed to hear such poets express phrases that overcame the ordinariness of existence, phrases more subtle than those of dogma or creed.

Marcebru had composed his poetry in the twelfth century, during the great age of teachers like Abelard, William of Saint-Thierry, and Saint Bernard, the founder of Cistercian monasticism. It was a time, too, when life in the castle was giving away to a more lavish life in the cities. Deprived of their feudal role as a shield against barbarian invasion, the old nobility was losing its financial supremacy, and much of its political strength, to an emerging merchant class whose wealth was already affecting the prosperity of towns such as Toulouse, Montpellier, and Marseilles.

As a result of their declining importance, the nobles often resorted to a life of profligacy. To them, marriage was no more than a business contract designed to secure territory or a family alliance. Thus, in the south of France, in a region known as *langue d'oc* (the land of yes), a spiritual lethargy had taken possession of the Church and heresy had spread into all corners of life. Such moral confusion, however, inevitably spawned a desire for a new and distinctive code of behavior. Love, that happiness attained through *jois,* was now seen as an ideal sought by all thoughtful people of the age.

Forbearance, patience, and refinement both in manners and in speech were regarded as the principal ingredients of courtly behavior. *Jovens*—that is, a youthful generosity of spirit—was also considered important to the attainment of *pretz,* or a courtly reputation. A person hoped to achieve a state of *valors,* a condition of innate moral worth that transcended even the Christian ethic. Moderation, too, was regarded a worthy attainment. Known as *mesura,* it was the ability to follow the course of action most suited to the demands of social and courtly convention in order to exploit the talents, aspirations, and qualities of the individual.

These were the noble ideals that had managed to seduce me as they had Marcebru, my poet. I thought of him as "my poet" in the knowledge that my recent adoption of him as a guide had marked me. I listened to his lyrics as I did my conscience: his voice had become the inner voice to which I had long refused to listen. The discovery of a death roll was as significant to me as the discovery of the Rosetta Stone must have been to Jean-François Champollion, the man who first deciphered the Egyptian hieroglyphs. He and I were in league with the mystery of language as a vehicle of discovery and growth.

Death rolls were a popular form of eulogizing on the death of important individuals from the ninth to fifteenth century in Europe. Normally written in Latin, the rolls were made of parchment and used by members of the religious orders to commemorate the recent death of an abbot or other much-loved cleric. In the hands of a wandering friar, such a document would travel about the region and be unraveled on some refectory table to receive a new consignment of words. In the course of a journey from monastery to monastery many a pious epitaph, poem, cogitation, or personal reminiscence would be added, thus creating a portrait of the deceased. A death roll was the final statement upon a person's life by those who knew him best.

How had such a document escaped detection in the Chapelle des Pénitents in Ussel all these years? More importantly, why was this death roll in the possession of Marcebru? Whose death was it dedicated to, anyway? These were the questions that immediately came to mind. I was enough of a sleuth to know that I was on the trail of something important. If one of the greatest poets of his age had chosen to make a penitential journey in memory of a friend, then whatever information this document imparted about the deceased would more than likely shed light on Marcebru's life, which until now had been hidden from view.

R.'s phone call had opened a door for me. Marcebru was calling, across time and out of the misty morning of death. He demanded my presence, among the worn and ravaged lava flows of the Dordogne, so heavy with the memory of ancient explosions. He wasn't dead after all, but merely languishing in some museum vault, a victim of neglect. This master of *entiers cuidars* (integrated thinking), who understood nature and what lies beyond it as a guide, had entranced me from the very beginning. I was his disciple and could only recite his words as if they were my own.

If nothing else, the existence of an undiscovered manuscript associated with the poet's life stimulated me more than I was prepared to admit. I had become conscious of a certain lassitude in my own behavior of late, a condition I reluctantly accepted as a part of growing older. Yet something inside me still wanted to reach out to the poet as a person who lived life more intensely, who saw things more clearly, and who was prepared to risk everything in the attainment of his goal. These values I still secretly admired, even if I had been forced to abandon them in my own life.

Refilling my glass with the wine of the poet, I resolved then to rescue his final testament from anonymity. Knowing that I had several weeks available before I was required to complete my monograph on Villon's poetry for publication, I felt it might be possible to take some time off to investigate the veracity of R.'s discovery for myself. It was at this point, late in the evening, that the rising sap of Marcebru's words moistened my lips:

Qe scienza jauzionda
M'apres c'al soleilh declin
Laus lo jorn, e l'ost'al matin,
Et a qec fol non responda
Ni contra musart no mus.

The knowledge that makes me rejoice
Teaches me to praise each day at sunset
And my host at dawn, and not to respond
To each and every fool that I meet,
Nor to gape at the stupid.

━━━

2

CONFERENCE
OF THE BIRDS

━━

PASSING THROUGH LONDON en route to Dover from my cottage in Hampshire, I stopped over to see an old friend, Horace Winterton, whose knowledge of French history was deep, if on occasions pedantic. He was, for example, of the opinion that Western art commenced with the Catalan fresco painters of northern Spain and culminated in the formal procession of Duccio's *Maesta* through the streets of Siena by an adoring public in 1308. He was adamant that any event after that represented a decline into secularism. This was something he couldn't abide—an art tainted by popular conceit.

German by birth, Horace had changed his name from Hermann Wintergarten before the outbreak of the war. He had done this, I suspect, to forestall any anguish he might have suffered in the wake of his country's defeat. Foreknowledge was one of his great strengths, as was his desire for anonymity. When he spoke it was always with a voice that conveyed his inherent thoughtfulness.

We met on a bright summer's day at a pub in Kew, on the River Thames. On the landing below stood seven white swans, their long necks gracefully reaching back over their bodies, suggesting a group of elderly men deep in discussion on issues of importance.

"Ah, it seems Plato's seven wise men have joined us," Horace remarked as we sipped our first pint of bitter.

"Even among birds, discussion is sometimes of the utmost relevance," I remarked, "just as it is for philosophers."

"As we know, troubadours were discoverers," Horace mused aloud, communing with the swans. "Their name, *trobador,* is derived from the verb *trobar,* which in modern French gives us the verb *trouver,* 'to find.' That makes a troubadour a composer of new melodies. He travels to regions that few of us are privileged to visit."

"Or dare," I added.

"Their ilk do not exist today. Imagine a band of poets wandering the byways of England, composing lyrics that would not only quicken the hearts of any self-respecting lovers but inspire them to seek after wisdom as well."

"Not in these times," I speculated. "Moral anarchism would be more appropriate."

"This is the language of our time. Dear friend, abandon such a temptation to interpret. Men like Marcebru worshiped the Virgin and extended their reverence to include all women. The cult of adoration of the female finds its origin in the worship of a goddess. Mary or Aphrodite, it matters little. These poets recognized an important truth lying behind the physical: that desire, under the influence of Platonic devotion, is capable of transforming love into art . . ."

"Which we know of today as the famous Laws of Love."

"Let us consider the pathology of such an emotion. The first effect of love is to produce a mental exaltation, a desire to lead a life worthy of the beloved. Troubadours referred to this as *joi d'amor.* Other virtues are produced under the influence of such an emotion. I assume all who have loved have experienced the joy of pleasing another. And also the feeling of self-restraint that ensues from such a heady encounter."

It seemed that medieval France had lost its ability to love. Too many wars, too many crusades to the

Holy Land, too many liaisons between ambitious kings and queens had left the land all but barren. People longed for virtue to reign over them once more. They wanted to hear the voice of reason and probity echo across their land, if only from the lips of poets.

"If I may, I would like to ask a favor of you when you reach those pleasant lands of Languedoc."

"Name your request, Horace," I invited.

"Invest your inquiry with a sympathy that extends beyond normal understanding. It may be that Marcebru wanted his death roll to remain a secret. Perhaps there are things in it that he did not wish to see the light of day, at least not while he was alive."

"Are you suggesting that he may have desired to withhold its contents from the world?"

"You are trying to interpret his motives again. Let us assume that Marcebru, a man of complex and obscure tonalities in all his utterances, had something important to say, but *for another time.* That time may well be now."

"By imputation, therefore, he was afraid of being misunderstood in his own time."

"Are not all fools, riddlers, and prophets?"

Meanwhile, the swans on the landing had begun to disperse. Uncurving their necks, they waddled down to the water's edge and proceeded to swim into the middle of the river. Without realizing it I became absorbed in their movements as they extended their wings and rippled the surface. Their symposium, it seemed, had ended.

———

3

THE LAND OF YES

—

Horace was an excellent informant with regard to twelfth-century life in the region now known as Aquitaine. Along with a number of other important poets, Marcebru had composed lyrics during the reign of Eleanor, the daughter of Duke William of Aquitaine, who is considered to be the first of the troubadours. Duke William's writings encapsulate a new spirit of chivalry and individualism that was often blasphemous, erotic, amoral, and sensitive. A great crusader, he is said to have painted a portrait of his mistress on his shield, remarking that it was his will to bear her in battle, as she had borne him in bed.

Eleanor, for her part, despite two disastrous marriages and numerous intrigues against her husbands, Henry II of England and Louis VII of France, became a great patron of the arts. According to Horace, she presided over the elevation of love to a new level of sensibility.

It was known as *fin' amors,* a distant love, and could be attained only by the renunciation of the immediate, close, and deceitful love that characterized normal relations between men and women. The profane ideal of happiness governed by the senses was transformed into a more refined form of love dominated by the imagination. Sensual love was overcome by reason. The yearning for a lady conforming to a beautiful, illuminating memory was what the troubadours attempted to celebrate in their poetry.

Horace insisted that this new sensibility, known as *gai saber* (gay science), had been inspired by feelings of resignation and despair among the aristocracy.

"People were bored with venality," he said. "They wanted something more, an imaginative possibility that only poetry could give. For the poets, who reflected such turmoil in their lyrics, absolute submission to love, to *Amors,* was considered the only way to happiness."

"A rocky path indeed."

"But one worth the risk. Arnaut Daniel, the minstrel from Périgord, said it most aptly." And Horace recited a few words:

> qu' Amors mi cuebr'e.m cela
> e.m fai tenir ma valor
> e.m capdela

>   Love overreaches and shelters me
>   Makes me hold fast to my virtue,
>   And gently acts as my guide.

"Love, it seems, began to replace chivalry as a code of behavior," I suggested.

"How else could one withstand an age bent upon reducing the smile to a frozen expression of deceit?"

"Were people so unhappy?"

"The Church was in decline, the Manichean heresy as practiced by the Cathars was on the rise, dualism was in the air. The old order was crumbling. It is strange how strictures on the intellect can have such devastating effect. Men of the north, at the bidding of the French king, were gathering to crush the heretical villages and towns of the south. Great clerics such as Saint Bernard and Saint Dominic were in the vanguard of this drive for orthodoxy, admonishing and cajoling wherever they went. This southern heresy caused shock waves throughout Christendom, for it suggested a freedom of thought inimical to the doctrines of the Church."

"People, I take it, were not yet ready to practice a genuine freedom of thought—at least, not during the era of the crusades."

"Culture had become monolithic," Horace continued. "The Church attacked its own kind, good men like Peter Abelard and Duns Scotus, unwilling to accept that people will always delight in a plurality of views. Theologians and clerics were obsessed with an ideal unity of belief extending throughout Christendom. They simply refused to accept that secular life might have something to offer. No wonder poetry began to thrive during those troubled times."

Poetry, caught up in the political turmoil of France eight hundred years ago, walked a narrow path between beauty and vagabondage as it attempted to reconcile people's best instincts. The celebration of love had become for many the inspiration they needed to break free from a life given over to worldly pursuits. Such a celebration had clearly inspired Marcebru's poetry.

"I half envy you," Horace admitted. "In Marcebru's death roll you have at your fingertips the ruminations of all those reflecting on the death of one of their own. It will be a peephole into their sadness. But it may be, like the rustle of alder leaves late in the afternoon, the suggestion of something invisible making its presence felt."

"I have some qualms at the prospect," I admitted.

"Fear is a part of your journey. It is up to you whether you choose to distance yourself from their pain, or embrace it as a friend."

And so we parted.

4

THE DEATH ROLL

—

MARCEBRU had clearly lived in times inspired by exhilaration and despair, fashioning his poems from the raw material of love. Survival was simple: enter the dungeon of the word, accept its restraints, and fly like a bird through its bars. Ascending to the high branches of the imagination was the only way to escape. There, he argued, freedom blossoms on a bough.

I was keenly awaiting my first encounter with his death roll the next morning. In Ussel that evening the church bells had seemed to toll in celebration of my arrival. R. had kindly left a note for me in the hotel lobby wishing me good luck and begging me to excuse his early departure. It appeared that the ruins of the nearby castle at Ventadour, old stones and sirens each one of them, had lured him away with their song.

As I looked through the window at the lights on

a bridge spanning a small stream below, I recalled some words of Marcebru that I had read: "The world of men is like a great orchard with shrubs, trees, and solid grafts. When they leaf and blossom they are like apple trees. Yet when they fruit they become like willow and alder: prodigal with promises but hard put to keep them."

It was typical of his uncompromising view. Of course I felt in sympathy with the man. Like him I had often asked myself why the idea of composure, of practicing a certain kind of physical restraint, was not considered important anymore. Obviously Marcebru had made peace with his own nature, otherwise he would not have associated himself with willow or alder. If, as trees, we find ourselves lopped or dead, who is to blame? Marcebru intimated that it was the axman in ourselves bent upon warring with our nature.

Who was this man? According to Horace, the facts are bare but fruitful. Born in Gascony, the son of a poor woman who was loved and then abandoned, Marcebru was left at the door of Lord Aldric del Vilar, who chose to take the infant into his home and bring him up as his own. As a foundling, a child conceived in the midst of a flawed passion who was later succored by an aristocrat, Marcebru moved between two worlds: the gutter and the salon.

Language, it seemed, was the only bridge between such worlds. Stretched to the limit by the need to come to terms with his life, he chose the poem as his bulwark. Marcebru projected himself on a number of levels, those of eloquence and on occasions anger when he chose to rail against the hypocrisy of his time. I couldn't blame him for that.

Ussel was a medieval town of turrets and coats of arms carved above doorways. In the morning I walked along its cobbled streets to the Chapelle des Pénitents, where the death roll was stored, trying hard not to hurry. A few people were sitting in corner cafés, drinking morning coffee and reading newspapers. I attempted to give off the air of a laurel leaf as I passed, calm yet full of vigor, patient yet alert. These were the qualities I felt I would need in the task ahead of me.

"Ah, you have come," the *chef de musée* welcomed me as I entered.

"Were you expecting me?" I asked.

"But of course. Your friend told me of your impending arrival. You are interested in the *rouleau de mort* of Marcebru."

"An unusual request, I know."

"In these times few are interested in the maundering of a poet."

Together we entered the main part of the building. Suits of chainmail and armor, halberds, two-handed swords, crossbows, and heraldic pennants hanging from the ceiling cluttered the wide corridor. We passed into the library, laden as it was with gold-embossed volumes, and crossed to a table where a scroll lay on a polished wooden frame.

"Here it is, monsieur. The object of your quest," the *chef de musée* announced.

The man unrolled the document. Water-stained and fragile, the parchment rather shakily revealed its contents. The first words rose like butterflies from the page, trembling and irresolute, pronouncing their solemn invocation: *Honorabiliter venerandis ac venerabiliter honorandis* (to the honor of venerable men, and the veneration of men of honor). These were the first words dedicated to someone who had died all those years ago, someone dear to Marcebru. I hardly dared touch the ravaged parchment.

"You see these water stains." The *chef de musée* pointed to the marks on the parchment. "They were caused by a strange incident. Legend has it the *rouleau de mort* was discovered by a shepherd downstream from Ussel while he was out looking for strays. It was a chill midwinter morning in 1196. What met him at the water's edge was a frozen landscape, blue and almost luminescent. The stream had iced over, causing a few branches to protrude like thorns.

"Then he noticed something strange glittering beneath the ice. Not bright, but more like a subdued glow, as if something were burning under the surface. He broke the ice with his staff. There, nestled among those chilly crystals, was the death roll that you see here. It had become a frozen object."

"It had been thrown into the river," I asked, "and the ice had somehow preserved it from deterioration?"

"Marcebru had chosen to abandon its destiny to the waters, it seems. For what reason we do not know."

"Possibly he tossed it from the bridge that I noticed from my hotel window."

"Such a question, monsieur, is beyond my capacity to answer. For the poet to have discarded what is clearly a heartfelt document is hard to fathom. But then—and this is only supposition on my part—perhaps he wished to transcend reason."

"You are ruling out foul play, impulsiveness, a moment of madness?"

"I rule out nothing. A *rouleau de mort* is a prolonged act of meditation—on death and all things that accompany it. When a man chooses to wander the roads of this varied and paradoxical region in pursuit of other people's memories, he engages in a conversation that goes beyond reason. He is asking someone to comment on the absence of another. For a poet this is his natural terrain. Yet there must come a time when even he draws back. He simply longs to forget."

The *chef de musée's* remarks struck me. There is a point reached when even the most courageous of men may experience fear—or perhaps dread. For such a man his wits, that sole preserve of his reason, may depart. Yet why should Marcebru draw back? I was confused.

"Much of the document is in Latin. Do you happen to speak the language?" the *chef de musée* asked.

"I'm a little rusty," I confessed.

"Fortunately for you a translation has been attempted by a Latin scholar here in town. He once taught at the University of Toulouse. The man has occupied his twilight years translating this document. From last report he has nearly completed it."

"He has done us all a great service," I replied.

"For him Latin is not a dead language, merely an ancient tongue that has chosen to take a nap."

The idea that a language might sleep conjured up vast dormitories of words, all snoring. I could hear them now, Assyrian, Sanskrit, Egyptian, the numerous languages of the Plains Indians, bloated Neanderthal verbs, armies of adjectives that had once belonged to the Mongols—all of them dreaming dreams. It seemed the scholar was an amateur philol-ogist, patiently translating the remnants of men's thoughts in an attempt to revive a dormant con-sciousness.

"Monsieur." The *chef de musée* aroused me from my own thoughts. "I suggest you visit this man. Talk to him. He lives in the only turreted house in Place Joffre. It is not hard to find."

"Are you sure he will receive me?"

"Why not? You are both in league with lost words."

The *chef de musée* rolled up the parchment and left the room.

———

5

A DISTANT LOVE

WHAT HAD MARCEBRU hoped to gain by surrendering his death roll to the river? Walking to the middle of the bridge in Ussel, I looked down at the silken thread of water flowing toward distant fields. I tried to picture him standing here on that winter's evening in 1196, his fingers loosening their grip on the document. Then, bobbing briefly in the chilly current, it was gone.

These ruminations were of little help. Perhaps the Latin scholar, heir to an ancient and fulfilled language, might point me in the right direction. I had nothing to lose by visiting him.

As the *chef de musée* had advised, his house was the only residence in the vicinity of Place Joffre with a turret. It reminded me of an inverted ice cream cone. On a brass plate above the door knocker was a phrase in Latin by Seneca. I finally managed to make a rough translation: "Live in accordance with your own nature."

"Instead we push one another into vices," I murmured, recalling Seneca's subsequent words.

Opening the door, the Latin scholar peered over his glasses as I introduced myself and explained the reason for my visit. Graying and slightly bent in his posture, he listened patiently, then invited me to enter. The man's voice radiated the rich sonority of Bible readings. It was not until after we had entered his study that I realized he possessed only one hand. The other had been substituted by a hook.

"Unfortunately, I lost it during the last war," he explained, sensing my unease. "I was never very competent at laying fuses."

"I presume you were a member of the French Resistance during the German occupation," I replied.

The scholar nodded.

"Those five fingers of mine have long since exclaimed their last. Now this curving steel fixture, immune as it is to pain, suffers every abuse that I can offer. I hold in deep affection its loyalty and inexhaustible resilience. It has served me without complaint all these years. Like language, its facility—and shall I say its utility?—has been refined by constant use. I hardly notice its existence anymore. But enough of this. You are interested in my partial translation of Marcebru's *rouleau de mort*. Such a strange request," the scholar added.

"Not so strange that you do not cherish it also," I suggested.

"That is because my life has been dedicated to tinkering with outmoded vehicles of communication. A linguistic mechanic, you may call me! I try to delve into old thoughts in the hope of discovering dormant sensibilities. As you know, under the bonnet of any language, particularly ancient ones, they say there is an engine waiting to roar into life. Exhilarating! All my caution as a scholar is tested by such reserves of vitality lying amid the machinery of discarded words. What I am looking for in my chosen language of study is the personality of those who have helped to formulate it in the first place."

"Men like Virgil, Ovid, Horace, even Thomas Aquinas," I suggested.

"The sensibilities of these men permeate Latin to the point where I hear them whispering to me, late at night, whenever I choose to open a book and allow their phrases to rise to my lips."

The scholar's hook cleaved the air as he spoke.

"Why Marcebru?" I inquired. "Though much of his death roll is in Latin, he himself wrote in Provençal."

"For no other reason than that his words spring

from Latin. His tongue evolved from men such as Virgil and Martial. He is their timeless echo."

Clearly the scholar had stepped into a superb world in which his thoughts and dreams had achieved an obligatory existence through the absence of others—those long-dead Latin poets and thinkers of the past. They were real to him, as real as if they were conversing with him in the forum. Through the prism of language he had recreated a rainbow of exquisite expression unknown to the rest of us, for he had made language timeless.

"I am somewhat at a loss," I found myself confessing. "Ever since I heard about Marcebru's death roll, I have wanted to know more about why he was acting as its messenger. What provoked one of the greatest poets of his age to embark upon a journey in memory of another? Who was that other person? It seems to me that the death roll endangers his reputation, as it alerts us to the possibility that he could find no words of his own to express how he felt. If a poet cannot express his pain, then what hope do the rest of us have of expressing our deepest emotions?"

"My response to your questions can only take the path of analogy," replied the scholar. "Consider Marcebru's silence as one would a knight who has recently returned from the Holy Land, after encountering the intransigence of opposing beliefs: Muslim against Christian, the age-old clash between the Trinity and Allah. Such conflicts make it more difficult for him to understand the nature of truth, and so he begins to doubt his own ability to believe. Faith is sundered. He longs for a time when questions were not asked. In that moment he loses his ability to discern, to articulate what was essentially a lie. He is left speechless, since all the old verities have fallen away."

"Doubt has consumed him, and so the ability to affirm is taken away," I ventured.

"For a poet, his whole being springs from affirmation. It is possible that Marcebru, because of his loss of faith, needed to ask others in order that he might regain his own."

"Through the death of another, perhaps."

The scholar smiled, pensively, half at me and half at some recollection of his own.

"The person to which you allude," he said, "was none other than a lady, Amedée de Jois, his *fin' amors*. She was the daughter of an aristocrat, and herself a woman of the veil."

"A nun?"

"So it seems."

This caught me by surprise. I had assumed that the subject of the death roll was a fellow poet or a member of his adopted family. Of course it was only natural that it should be a woman, since most troubadours found their inspiration in the distant worship of love in the person of the wife of a noble. What seemed strange in Marcebru's case was that he had chosen to address his feelings to someone who, in theory, was even more unapproachable: a bride of the church. How could he express his feelings through such an impossible love?

"So he journeyed about the countryside, visiting monasteries and hermitages, castles and churches, taverns and hostelries, in the hope that others might shed light on what was most distant from him," I suggested.

"It seems that Marcebru chose to adore the embodiment of an ideal in Amedée de Jois."

"Much as Dante had done through Beatrice."

"Your task, monsieur, will be to investigate the sources of this document in order to discover why he tossed it into the stream, and why after that he disappeared from the pages of history. We know nothing of his last years. The true mystery of Marcebru lies in the way he discarded his love, his persona, and his presence on the bridge that winter's evening. Until we know, he will haunt Ussel like a ghost, forever tantalizing people like you and me. We long to know what constituted his essence, not as a historical personage, though that is interesting too, but as an expression of language. You see, he moved within the domain of the word. This was his country, his realm. His silence on the matter is our despair.

"To that end, monsieur, I would like to give you all the work I have so far completed on the death roll. In your hands there is a chance you may discover information that I cannot. I have gone to much pain to translate the document, pouring out many years of unconjugating Latin and obscure Provençal verbs into its realization. Now I understand why. A foreigner such as yourself and a man with distance on your side, you are the only one who can possibly unravel this mystery, since you are relatively detached. I'm afraid that I am too close. The solitude of this turret has imprisoned me in the memory of Marcebru and the thoughts of his friends. Let others, those that you meet along the way—let them illuminate the more obscure passages of the text, and so unveil the real Marcebru. I have grown to accept that all of us can possess but a portion of the mystery, no more."

My host produced from a cabinet a scroll of paper that had been fashioned to look remarkably like the death roll I had witnessed in the Chapelle des Pénitents.

"Take it, my friend," he said, offering me the document. "What you have here is but the beginning of a journey, the first milestone."

I thanked the scholar. My hands trembled with anticipation as I held the translation of Marcebru's death roll. Here at last was a copy of the memories of all those who had spoken to him, now so carefully collected and recorded. Already I sensed that I was entering uncharted territory. Marcebru, my sibling, had tendered me his hand.

———

6

A CLERK'S
CONFESSION

——

THE PRECIOUS DOCUMENT was in my possession at last. I felt a sense of exhilaration, almost of victory, knowing that Marcebru's death roll now lay before me on the table by the window that overlooked the bridge of Ussel. It was as if the roll had risen from the waters.

At first I made no attempt to read its contents. I chose instead to ponder Marcebru's movements on that chill winter's eve. Had he too much to drink in a tavern? Was the wound of Amedée's death too painful to staunch? Did he regret not being by her side at her death? Questions scuttled back and forth, all rodents longing to find some tasty morsel.

Marcebru had spent his life confronting humankind's greatest challenge: how to find a more acceptable way of choosing between the "whole way" and the "fragmented way," a theme explored in so many of his poems. "Faced with these different ways of thinking," I recalled him saying in one of his statements, "I am deeply concerned to separate the fragmented way from the whole way. I consider man to be, through God, at one with nature, which can be a guide in discriminating between various ways of thinking."

Here was a man wedded to the task of discernment to the point where many often considered his work a little confused. One of his contemporaries, the poet Peire d'Alvarnhe, suggested that some people regarded Marcebru as stupid because he did not understand his own nature, nor for what reason he was born. Nonetheless his *dreitura,* or uprightness, fascinated Peire as much as it did me. Marcebru was aware that his bid to achieve a natural form of composition in his poems often exposed him to the mockery of his fellow troubadours. He confessed as much in one of his poems:

> Pursuing the art of natural composition
> I carry the flint, tinder, and steel,
> While paltry poets, mindless hornets all of them,
> Turn my song into a yawn and ridicule it.

His was a lonely road. Whether by choice or otherwise, Marcebru had been forced to travel along it for much of his life. Perhaps, as a foundling and counterfeit aristocrat, there had been no other alternative but to embark upon a career as a troubadour, since the legitimacy of birth had been denied him. In poetry, in the supreme legitimacy of the word, he had sought protection from the barbs of denial.

Gazing at the bridge below, I sensed that in Marcebru a new spirit had found its home, one that asked him to explore through the medium of language the full depth and range of his feelings, however truculent or morbid they might turn out to be. Not that those feelings had become embodied in words; rather, such was the intensity of his experience that only through words could his feelings achieve a vitality, and a life, outside himself.

Marcebru became the patron of the *trobar clus* or "closed" style of writing. This entailed the interweaving within a poem of more than one level of meaning, and the gradual revealing, to the observant listener, of the hidden treasure lying below its surface. It was a style of poetry that intimated the existence of a certain moral truth. Many troubadours despised the use of such a technique, however, arguing instead for a clear style that relied on the simple beauty of the poem's surfaces.

For Marcebru, writing in the *trobar clus* style severely limited his audience. Those who regarded

poetry as little more than a courtly entertainment
were often troubled by the meaning in his verse. His
poems could lead unwary listeners into a morass of
moral subtlety from which they may not have been
able to extricate themselves. Nor was Marcebru in
any mood to spare them from such trials. For those
ready to take up the challenge, Marcebru wanted his
work to be regarded as something concrete, a bridge
over which they could cross. If they chose to jump off
it before reaching the far side, that was their problem. "Our citadel cannot fall to the assaults of bad
poetry," is the way he put it, adapting a line from his
beloved Boethius.

Perhaps the reason why he chose to abandon his
great love to the waters lay in the death roll itself. Unraveling a portion of it on the table in my hotel room,
I realized at once that because of the way the death
roll had been arranged, the last words came first. The
choice that lay before me was whether to follow the
route of the death roll forward from the Abbey Saint-
Martin, high in the Pyrenees, in the footsteps of
Marcebru, or backward from Ussel where he disappeared. Whichever choice I made, the opportunity of
absorbing the remarks of all whom he met in the spirit
in which they were uttered was too much to resist.

In the end, the decision was made for me by the
death roll itself. When I read the last recorded entry in

the text, written by one Willelmus, a clerk who had
presumably provided Marcebru with shelter for the
night in Ventadour prior to the poet visiting Ussel, I
recognized at once that his poem was as enigmatic as
his guest's. Clearly at home in the *trobar clus* style also,
Willelmus had couched his thoughts about Amedée
de Jois in the language of thorns. These remarks, cou-
pled to my own curiosity, compelled me to begin my
journey where Marcebru's had ended, if only because
I wanted to know what had happened there. I read:

> Touch her hem, on it phrases are filigree.
> There is more to life than death.
> She whom you once knew, loved, and
>   quenched
> As a flame too hurtful to bear
> Has now become a funeral pyre.
> Grant her audience, but as a maid in whom
> All the beauty of cessation palpitates
> Like coals in a tripod outside Apollo's hall.

Was this the bitter conclusion of a tortuous journey through memory, love, and its loss? Or was it, as
I was starting to suspect, the renewal of an ancient liaison with the word itself?

━━━

7

AMONG THE RUINS

—

ARMED with these cryptic remarks from the death roll, I took a bus to the village of Moustier, where I proceeded on foot to the castle of Ventadour. I had no reason to believe that I would find anything there except ruins, but it was my only lead. If Willelmus had lived nearby and had sheltered Marcebru during his wanderings, then the great gorges of Luzege, set among a wild and impregnable landscape, might yet provide me with some clue.

The castle was the birthplace of another famous troubadour, Bernard of Ventadour. The son of a baker, he was a notable exponent of the *trobar leu*, or "simple" style of poetry despised by Marcebru. Peire d'Alvarnhe, a fellow troubadour, ridiculed him as being the son of a serving man, with a mother who did little more than heat the oven and gather twigs. Yet

Bernard was much admired for the lightness of his touch and his submission to the more purely romantic side of love. He was patronized by Eleanor of Aquitaine and Henry II, who invited him to attend their coronation in Westminster Abbey in 1154. He, like many of his contemporaries, remained under the spell of Cupid's darts as depicted by Ovid in his erotic love poems, *Amores*.

The path to the ruins smelled oddly of acorns. There were no oak trees about, but the flinty stones and wide view of the Luzege Gorges intimated the color and hardness of those seeds. I felt invigorated by the walk, as if I had stumbled upon the inspiration for one of Marcebru's poems. When he spoke of the rough season of tempests and the season of dryness, I sensed the sterility that often clouded his vision. Here at Ventadour the crumbling walls murmured uneasy refrains as a light breeze passed through them, causing the heather to quiver on the slopes nearby.

On a saddle of the hillside overlooking the crumbling walls I noticed a figure dressed in a black cape, beret, and pointed boots. The figure stood before an easel painting a landscape, a palette of oils in one hand. Drawing nearer, but not so as to disturb the artist at work, whose back was turned toward me anyway, I watched the deft movement of brush against canvas. It turned out that the artist was a woman, in her early sixties perhaps, judging by a gray hair bun neatly pinned back beneath her beret.

Some minutes passed before I engaged her in conversation. I don't know why I felt so emboldened, except to say that her austere appearance gave me confidence. Gazing at her reminded me of dolmens standing in some prehistoric sanctuary. She stood there, a view of Ventadour's ruined battlements her sole object of veneration.

Her back still to me, the woman responded courteously to my inquiries about her work. She made a practice, it appeared, of wandering from one ruin to another in the region, looking for what she called "the language of battlements." When I asked her to explain what she meant by this remark, the woman spoke of ruins possessing a poetry of their own. I asked her whether she was familiar with the troubadour tradition in Aquitaine, and whether she might have heard of Marcebru. To my surprise her brush pursued without pause the images on her canvas.

"Such men stood outside their time," she remarked, her voice melodious yet tinged with a sadness that comes from a rich inner life.

"Poetry, by its nature, condemns the poet to exile," I suggested.

Meanwhile, I produced the death roll from my backpack and read aloud the lines by Willelmus as a way of providing food for our discussion.

"Monsieur," the landscape painter observed, dipping her brush into the gray color on her palette. "The woman he refers to is both Amedée de Jois and another; Sophia, I believe, she was called by the ancients. She represents the illumination of the intelligent mind bent upon discovering the proper constitution of nature. Willelmus recognized in Marcebru's loss something more profound than the simple sadness evoked by her death. Perhaps the poet lost the gift of being more than himself, and so allowed Amedée's death to darken his palette."

"What sort of person do you think Amedée de Jois was?"

"I know nothing of her life. But if Marcebru's dedication to her memory is anything to go by, then she possessed extraordinary qualities. Amedée de Jois embodied a yearning that she imparted to the poet. He, in turn, regarded her as someone in whom he could place his trust. She shared with him her solicitude, her deep, abiding, and yet productive *unease*. Does this sound absurd? Of course I'm only thinking aloud.

"Willelmus likens her to a flame, a hot coal flickering in Apollo's tripod. Obviously she glowed. The poem you recited asks Marcebru to see Amedée de Jois, not as dead, but as someone capable of suffering along with him. However tragic her death might have been, it was to guide him in his wanderings. She wanted him to believe that his time on earth could be infused with the hope that one day he might become master of himself, his craft, and so create a work that transcended itself. Is not this the true task of a poet?"

"I believe so," I admitted.

"All of us, I think, must adhere to this desire in whatever way we can. As a painter I try to imbue my landscapes with qualities that overcome reality. Of course it is difficult; one must be on guard against too strong a desire to change reality. But then, some of us are blighted in a way that makes it impossible to see the world as it really is. This may have been Amedée de Jois's difficulty, who knows?"

The artist stood back from her easel, and for the first time I was able to see her canvas more fully. She had not painted the ruins of Ventadour castle as it stood before us, but as the castle that Bernard, Willelmus, and even Marcebru might have known. With a sure sense of the past, the woman had rendered an imaginary castle of impregnable walls, vistas, and heraldic flags fluttering on its ramparts.

At this point the landscape painter turned to face me, her cocked beret and dark cape accentuating the whiteness of her face. She wore dark glasses, the kind that blind people often favor when they wish to conceal their vacant gaze. All along, this blind woman had been painting an interior landscape. Through her the castle had been rebuilt even more grandly than before.

"In a sense, monsieur, Amedée de Jois is like me, a victim of a lifelong wound."

"But you see the world as it *could* be," I replied, awed by her dexterity and her keen sense of the castle's invisible architecture.

"It is the only way I know how to make up for what I lack," the artist replied.

In those few moments of illumination the castle stood before us, a transfigured ruin.

———

8

PALIMPSEST

Marcebru's death roll had yielded its first fruits. I felt that Amedée de Jois had accompanied me on my trek to Ventadour. I had touched her hem, felt the filigree in her heart. Yet her enigma remained. It seemed that I was at the mercy of a text whose meaning was revealed to me only through the thought of others.

This woman was essential to my investigation, since it was she who had inspired Marcebru to make his journey. To understand her place in his life I needed to study the death roll closely. What special quality did she bestow upon the poet other than being for him the embodiment of an elusive love? Certainly it takes more than wisdom or truth to enliven a man's heart.

I returned to my hotel in Moustier to consider my next move. On the bed I unraveled the death roll and began to read it. I became an archaeologist, sifting through its debris. The words were like shards from a painted vase recently unearthed—the complete image could only be imagined. A portion of some toga, an arm, a horse's hoof perhaps, these were all I possessed.

Of course these were personal reflections, not dead thoughts—none of them. They were the breath of inspiration of men and women who were connected in various ways to Amedée de Jois and to Marcebru. They too had shared with him their dream of origin, however faint that vision might have been. Like Amedée and Marcebru, they participated in the mystery of not knowing why they had acted as they did. Whether it was a Geraldus, a Petrus, a Frater Udalardus, or a Sister Olivia, and all those others whom Marcebru had asked to write down their thoughts—they all had one thing in common: that inner struggle to realize a person closest to his heart.

It became necessary to immerse myself in their words, drown in their collective speech. Abbots and abbesses, monks and nuns, knights and Hospitalers, milkmaids and vintners, cask makers and swordsmiths, friars and clerks, lords and their ladies, each had crossed Marcebru's path as he journeyed through Aquitaine, through the kingdom of Oc. They were the voices of their time, of all those attempting to

make sense of the senseless: the death of an extraordinary woman who had died in the prime of her life.

I began to read at random, pausing after each
statement to contemplate its meaning:

> "She held courage and silence awakened,"
> one Guilelmus from the monastery of Savi-
> gny wrote. "The good Amedée de Jois, late
> of Abbey Saint-Martin-du-Canigou, called
> upon herself to reject happiness in pursuit of
> victory. Aquitaine mourns the stillness of her
> bell."

> "Carry with you, Marcebru," wrote friar
> Bernardo of the Abbey Notre Dame des
> Chateliers, "the knowledge that Nature is
> content with few and little. If you try
> to press superfluous additions upon what is
> sufficient for Nature, your bounty will di-
> minish. Remember that absence contains
> within it not emptiness, but the obligation
> we all must adopt toward memory."

> "Marcebru, abandon this hair shirt of an-
> guish that you wear," announced Johannis,
> an armorer from Puy the poet had met on
> the road. "Your sword is the word. Why, is it

not buried in the blade itself? Brandish it bravely, soldier. The death of Amedée de Jois is no more than a skirmish. You must partake of her demise yourself, cross Styx in a coracle of hope, utter one word that will drain it of its ferment."

———

"It is dangerous country that you traverse. What matters to you, Marcebru, is never to lack the courage to explore its outer limits," wrote a fellow troubadour from the court in Poitiers, traveling to Albi to take up a position with his new patron.

Finally I read a short poem written by titulis sancti Cecilia, abbess of the priory of Saint-Jean-Baptiste, alluding to Amedée's death:

> Contemplate God in the worm.
> Know that in its entrails He lies,
> A limbless serpent of earth.
> As the worm feeds on the dead
> So does He satisfy His hunger
> Through her, delicious banquet of grief.

Here was my first real foray into this frozen orchestra of words; and how the notes burned their dark melody in my mind! The landscape painter was right: gray is the color of ruin. The question remained whether I were capable of climbing back beyond original memory, over time's contribution to it, and enter the preserve of their inspiration. Somewhere among these eulogies lay an erasure, a palimpsest, upon which was inscribed Marcebru's own deepest yearnings.

Damn him! Already Marcebru was leading me astray. His hiddenness was weaving its magic. He was a man without city, occupying no specific place, alone, strange and without issue, unstructured and at times unordered, living within some inner design known only to himself. He had set himself the task of surviving inside the poem, inhabiting language like a specter, losing himself in the beauty and nuance of a perfectly expressed line. How I envied him! He was a man in possession of some secret that he was struggling to make real. What was it? What had caused him to dedicate his last days to an epitaph?

At Ventadour that day I had witnessed a ruin. The painter had managed to rebuild it for me, stone by stone. It was up to me to rebuild Marcebru's life, gather together all the rubble of his inner experience and arrange it so that he might once more stand alone.

9

THE DIVINE NAMES

—

REREADING THESE REMARKS from the death roll the next morning, I remembered Horace's warning that Marcebru's character could not be studied in isolation. Marcebru was a man of his time, in concert with ideas and prejudices that had flourished around refectory tables and in the hallways of cathedral schools like those of Chartres, Poitiers, and Paris. Even if he hadn't personally visited these places or heard the great teachers expounding their thoughts, he would have picked up the drift of their ideas from others.

In his poetry he often alluded to the Holy Land and to Spain. Outremer, or the region of Palestine, appears in his work both as a place and a metaphor for a lost paradise occupied by unbelievers. It is likely that he visited Cyprus and Acre, possibly even skirted the walls of Jerusalem during his travels. I knew that

he had journeyed to Spain in the hope of finding patronage at its courts. In spite of his dislike of Islam he
had absorbed many of its ideas without knowing it,
much as the Templars had done lazing about on di-
vans in Outremer. Arab theologians were saturated in
Greek thought, and thus with Neoplatonism, which
in turn had fueled the fires of the medieval mind.

Prominent among these thinkers was Saint
Denys, or Dionysius the Areopagite, as he was origi-
nally known. His works had been translated into
Latin by Hilduin, abbot of Saint-Denis, whose patron he became. Later John Scotus Erigena, an Irish
cleric, fell under the spell of Saint Denys's writings,
propounding his ideas in two masterworks, *De divi-
sione naturae* and a commentary on Saint Denys's
Celestial Hierarchy. Such was the power and beauty of
the monk's ideas that it lured John Scotus into dangerous waters. He began to propound a view of God,
and of his creation, that was in part pantheistic and
so potentially heretical.

"There is, I hold," Horace had said, quoting
John Scotus, "nothing visible or corporeal that does
not signify the invisible and the incorporeal." The
physical world, Scotus argued, could not be known
in its essence because it was the cause of nothing. But
it could signify an invisible world, the source of divine Ideas, and thus attain to a status of beauty un-

equaled. God reveals himself through nature by way of a so-called theophany. Nature must therefore be regarded as the mirror of God. Such ideas, drawn from the pages of Saint Denys, and by implication the harsh deserts of Arabia where intuition and reason were often inseparable, and where this obscure Syrian theologian had nurtured his vision in the first place, imparted a mysticism to all who came under their spell.

I was alerted to this fact by the statements in Marcebru's death roll of both Guilelmus of Savigny and the armorer from Puy. The former had suggested that Amedée de Jois may have voluntarily chosen death as a way of overcoming the balefulness of nature. Johannis had gone further by suggesting that Marcebru should partake of his love's demise also, "cross Styx in a coracle of hope," as he so succinctly put it. Both remarks intimated that victory, the reestablishment of a primitive state of wholeness, could be achieved only through the act of dying. Their remarks conformed with John Scotus's belief that the return of all creatures to God started with death.

These were indeed choppy waters to be sailing! The word as sword indicated how such a death could be realized: that language, the power and beauty of a poem, may well lead to the perfect death. All of

Marcebru's informants so far had intimated that the "dangerous country" of the word should be explored to its "outer limits." No one, not least the poet, could erase memory. The obligation for everyone was to shore up emptiness by way of an abiding commitment to expression.

Was Marcebru's secret ambition to write the perfect poem? Had he, until the death of Amedée, believed that this power belonged to him alone? Did pride enter the equation? Numerous questions remained unanswered, yet I suspected Marcebru's decision to toss away the death roll was irrevocably linked to them. A man who breathed through poetry as a fish does through gills would surely not wish to stifle his voice by such an act of censorship—unless, of course, he had discovered a better way of expressing himself.

These were perplexing thoughts. I was aware of the danger of using psychological techniques to analyze the poet's behavior. Thankfully he resisted all my imputations to reduce his actions to such facile motives. Because his actions were so completely themselves, so mysterious, so bathed in the gestures of the olive tree rather than willow or alder, I gained the impression that he was utterly himself only when railing against the hypocrisy of his age and the failure of the aristocracy to live up to those high expectations invested in it by fate.

But what of Amedée de Jois, whose death had inspired him to descend from his Olympian solitude to seek out the expression of others? The temptation, of course, was to rush to Abbey Saint-Martin where she had died, and confront her enigma head on, rather than wander about the countryside as I was doing. That would be too easy. A mystery was imbedded in Marcebru's journey that could not be easily discounted. To dismiss it would be as if to shoot a bird in flight: the bird would tumble to earth and so relieve the sky of the strange beauty of gravity being defied. Marcebru's pilgrimage was an act of defiance, an attempt to challenge and overcome a deeply felt anger—or was it hurt?

The idea that he may have striven to write the perfect poem intrigued me. This was not so unusual, as poets have always believed in the power of language. Many would regard Homer's *Iliad,* the Hindu Upanishads, or the Norse Njal sagas as examples of how the world is transformed by the beauty of the word. A detonation, an explosion of sound and thought at the heart of the intellect, is basic to human nature. From the poet's point of view, and that of his listeners too, the world is a better place at the conclusion of every recital.

This was Marcebru's chosen path. He had wandered the world in pursuit of experience in order to fashion his songs. That the world fell short of his expectations was a part of his quandary, and his glory. He saw what others chose to ignore. The rule of Love, of *fin' amors,* demanded he be vigilant in his pursuit of excellence. Frustrated, disgruntled, and at times at odds with the world and himself, Marcebru nevertheless wrung from it what he wanted: the stuff of song, the pure flame of outpouring that would remain forever a part of consciousness.

I admired him for that. But then, I also felt a strong desire to distance myself from his demands, believing that they were in some way luring me toward some unforeseen danger. Perhaps Amedée de Jois had felt as I did. Perhaps she had chosen to escape his influence. Perhaps love—and I had to assume that their relationship was founded upon an intimacy of some sort, even if it were a distant love—hadn't been enough to sustain them.

I began to suspect that I had stumbled upon a relationship more complex than any I had imagined. Marcebru and Amedée de Jois may well have plumbed love to the point where the only alternative for them was to exclude life altogether. Guilelmus intimated as much when he wrote that Amedée de Jois had chosen to reject happiness in pursuit of victory. But did she, in death, turn her back on Marcebru?

How my thoughts had become a jumble! I had embroiled myself in Marcebru's time, in his love, in his pilgrimage through the old land of Oc, each step now leading me further into this maze. I had to ask myself whether what lay beyond these twists and turns was the knowledge that Amedée de Jois's abandonment of earthly love may have been but a prelude to a more elaborate deceit.

━━━

10

A COUNTRY WALK

I RETURNED FROM A WALK that afternoon to find a message from R. waiting at reception. He had phoned during my absence, and the concierge had kindly written it down. I read his cryptic words: "Go to Rocamadour, to Place Saint-Amadour, where you will find a shop selling fine-quality paper. Ask for M. Poulen, the papermaker. He has information significant to your quest." That was all.

R.'s elusiveness was irritating. We were friends, but even friends should not press one another's patience too far! Nonetheless, his advice had come at an opportune moment. The names of hostelries and abbeys between Moustier and Rocamadour mentioned in the death roll made little sense, as most of them had disappeared from any map. This sudden leap to Rocamadour, though startling for Marcebru, who had traveled on foot, seemed altogether too abrupt to me also—unless I chose to walk there my-self.

Which is what I decided to do. I made my way along country lanes from village to village, stopping overnight in sleepy hotels where I enjoyed hearty meals, which quickly restored me after my daily treks. By the Dordogne River I took advantage of its beauty to sit and meditate on the words in the death roll. Near Saint-Cyprien I stopped over to view the Chapelle de Rodon l'Espi, a sober Romanesque church whose name is reputedly based on the Latin expression *rotondo spino,* in honor of a reliquary from the Crown of Thorns.

Market towns such as Sarlat welcomed me with their produce; abbey churches and castles radiated their ancient marvels, their solicitude and slight sense of menace. Medieval frescoes on refectory walls, arcades of columns around village squares, limestone bluffs and Gothic bishoprics, a statue of Adam and Eve entwined by a serpent, a tapestry of Saint Martin on horseback slicing his cloak with a sword, and pigs being led along lanes like mules—all these impressions filled my days as I made my way toward Roca-madour. At Martel I made a diversion to observe the crest of the three hammers fluttering on flagpoles in memory of Charles Martel, who defeated the Moors at Poitiers in 732.

Is this not what journeys are for: to enter the memory of people and places? I began to revel in the solitude it granted me. The Dordogne that week became an outlet for some interesting thoughts: the more I studied the death roll, the more I found myself confusing the landscape I was journeying through with the words of its previous inhabitants. Place and person had become one.

Memorable too was the afternoon I lay down to rest under an old tree and produced the death roll from my backpack. The words that flowed were as limpid as the stream nearby. Once more Marcebru's friends rose up to greet me, fish entranced by the sky, bearing with them hidden depths.

"I entreat you, Marcebru," wrote a cloth merchant from Saint-Cyprien, "attend to the duality of waste that you bear. Evil exists, even if you fail to acknowledge his handshake. The death of a loved one, while painful, can be a gift. Such a death may help you disentangle yourself from this world. There's an old eagle in you, its wings bare of feathers, yet still capable of gliding from its aerie. Cling to its talons! The flight you attempt may yet have the quality of a piece of Ghent cloth. All I ask is that you not fail to let go before it chooses to abandon you on high."

━━━

"Rudel's love may inspire you as death was its outcome," one Bertran wrote, "But remember, his distant love took the veil and quit this world. I say to you: sing of your anguish. Make of it a poem that unearths new treasures for us all."*

━━━

"No man is so completely happy that something somewhere does not clash with his condition," wrote Gauzbert, a hermit whom Marcebru had met living in the forest of Bessede, quoting a line from Boethius. "I urge you to abandon your deliberations on

---

* The troubadour Jaufré Rudel (d. 1148) fell in love with the countess of Tripoli without ever seeing her, solely from reports he received from pilgrims returning from Antioch. Wanting to meet her, he took the cross and sailed to Tripoli. Unfortunately he fell ill on board, and was carried ashore a stricken man. Hearing of his plight, the countess came to his bed and took him in her arms. Realizing who she was, Rudel recovered enough to praise God for having allowed him to see the object of his love. Then he died in her arms. So grieved was the countess that she took the veil shortly after Rudel was buried. The story of Rudel inspired Robert Browning to pen his classic love poem *Rudel to the Lady of Tripoli*.

the absence of another. You will come to accept that her death is rooted in bliss. By the Holy Shroud of Cadouin, I tell you there is room for you in heaven if you break with remorse and follow your instincts. *She* is your gate."*

———

"Outremer has left its scars," a Knight of Saint John counseled, recently returned from Palestine. "I saw men there, some of them poets, sorely affronted by the infidel sword. To them, death tasted of sherbet since they had been granted an indulgence by our holy Pope. Damn him for granting what was not his to give! Their blood, spilled on the slopes of Calvary, mingled with that of Our Lord's. One who fell beside me, and who still had breath enough, whispered his last request in my ear: 'Tell Marcebru, if your paths should

---

* The shroud of Cadouin, a piece of linen cloth brought from Antioch by a priest from Périgord, was believed to have been wrapped around Christ's head at the time of his crucifixion. It was an object of pilgrimage during the middle ages. In 1934, and later in 1982, research concluded that the embroidered bands were characteristic of the artwork produced during the Fatamid dynasty of the late 11th century. Thus the Holy Shroud was denuded of its miraculous properties by scientific tests.

cross, that he of all the troubadours gave us the truth of *fin' amors*. I die with his song on my lips.'

———

"I tell you, my friend, bold knight of the word, with this support you have the opportunity to conduct a counterattack. Those who give their lives in defense of Jerusalem have your songs in their hearts. You entrance them, is this not enough? Put a sword to your keening, bury the cold towers of Saint-Martin under a rubble of words. It is your only defense."

I read no more that afternoon but savored these words—thoughts written long ago, yet filled with a passion as if they had been expressed only yesterday. I felt I knew the cloth merchant, the hermit Gauzbert, Bertran, and the Knight Hospitaler returning home from Palestine, so directly did they speak. They argued a case that fell on ears sensitive to their cause. Marcebru, they seemed to be saying, do not allow your own pain to come between you and destiny. The poem is a fortress: lay down your life for it (as others had done in Outremer), but never surrender to the enemy. The three hammers of Charles Martel are clamoring for your victory just as they did at Poitiers.

These four eulogies, simply expressed and so personal, only intensified my interest. Amedée de Jois had much to answer for, it seemed. If the most acerbic tongue of his age had chosen to remain mute in the face of such words from the death roll, then clearly something serious and strange must have occurred. Had Marcebru killed someone? Had his father denounced Marcebru to the world because of his criticism of the aristocracy? Or had Amedée de Jois spurned his love as being that of a man above his station?

Captive to this medieval drama myself, I began to look for answers in the most unlikely places. The people I met on the road, the village squares I sat in to take refreshment of an afternoon, even the clock towers I heard tolling at midday, they all taunted me with their as yet hidden part in the drama. Everything was implicated in some way—an absurd thought, but no less real for being so.

I had invited Marcebru to relive his experiences and so inflict his silence upon me. Now I was powerless to lay him to rest.

———

II

THE WATERMARK

—

Home to the legendary Black Madonna, a miraculous Virgin painted in the rustic style, Rocamadour is a town whose medieval origins lend themselves to altered states of consciousness. To climb the steps of Via Sancta is to experience a mild form of levitation: breathlessness and a sense of awe at the prospect of viewing saint's bones in the company of pilgrims who have struggled up there on their knees. It is enough to impress the most skeptical mind.

According to legend, in 1166 a local inhabitant had expressed a wish to be buried under the threshold of the Chapel of the Virgin, but during excavations for his tomb the body of the hermit Zaccheus was discovered. So old was the grave that some suggested it might be the body of an Egyptian hermit from the third century. His bones inspired a number of miracles, which drew people from all over France. Henry II, one of the first to kneel before the tomb, was cured of a painful sword wound. Not to be outdone, a procession of kings and queens soon followed. Pilgrims by the thousands took up the staff and journeyed to Rocamadour on their way to Santiago de Compostela.

The town is attached to the rock face like a starling's nest. Once I had struggled up the Great Stairway it felt as though I too had flown all the way from Africa on one of their migrations. With the address that R. had given me in hand, I passed through the ramparts to find myself in a square surrounded by medieval churches and some small shops.

Under an arcade I noticed a shop selling fine-quality paper, its corniced windows offering a display of handcrafted sheets and envelopes. I studied their uneven elegance through the glass, marveling at the way they invited the onlooker to write down his innermost thoughts. My curiosity aroused, I opened the door.

A man, in his early seventies perhaps, stood behind a glass-topped counter. He wore a white shirt with a Victorian collar. Armbands above the elbows drew back the cuffs to expose his wrists. He peered over a pair of pince-nez balanced on his nose. Though severe in appearance, the man managed to radiate a benign air. He reminded me of a figure in an illuminated manuscript, so composed and deliberate was his demeanor.

I explained the nature of my visit, outlining my trek from Moustier in the footsteps of Marcebru. M.

Poulen listened. He seemed surprised that I, a foreigner, had taken up the task of solving the riddle of Marcebru's *rouleau de mort*.

"Such an interesting journey," M. Poulen remarked, removing his glasses and placing them on the counter. I glanced through their lens, catching a glimpse of a watermark in a sheet of paper in the cabinet below. It depicted an ancient amulet, the kind found in the Middle East.

"Already I have seen a great deal that has impressed me, and have had some unusual encounters," I admitted.

"It is those invisible things that accost us more than we acknowledge. I know myself, whenever I am trying to fashion a piece of paper out of coarse materials, I always hope that the result of my labors will turn out to be an object of beauty. Such is the nature of all journeys. They take us through the unthinking events, routines, frustrations, and disappointments of the day—only to lead us to the discovery that something remarkable has occurred: one is surprised by a certain form, largely intuitive, that suddenly appears—none other than the completion of a task."

"You acquire such an insight from the manufacture of paper?"

"Do not underestimate the humble page," M. Poulen gently admonished. "Without it, where would we be? More importantly, where would the word reside? It is one of the greatest inventions. On its flatness, its blankness, and sometimes its whiteness, the word lands like a swan. Paper is the lake upon which those majestic birds of thought come to rest, there to inspire us with their elegance, their charm, and their substance. Monsieur, paper is also the bed of language. We sleep on it and we dream."

M. Poulen had hardly drawn breath during his monologue. It was as if he had been rehearsing it for my benefit.

"It's obvious, M. Poulen, that you have a profound respect for your craft."

"As did Marcebru, I'm sure."

"Yet so far as we know, he wrote no other song after the death of Amedée de Jois."

"But that is not to say he never again composed an *invisible* poem. Take this piece of parchment," M. Poulen went on to explain as he removed a sheet of paper from a shallow box on the bench behind him. "To the casual eye it seems like a blank piece of paper. But if you look closely, you will see a watermark buried in its texture."

I studied the paper. A faint image of a heraldic couple, possibly a king and queen, were realized in the fashion of characters in a Tarot deck. They looked faintly Oriental. At the same time I tried to picture them as representing Marcebru and Amedée de Jois, two figures implacably frozen in their expressions, and yet somehow full of life.

"They stand for the regal power of thought," M. Poulen added, "and come from a distant land, far from the familiarity of our lives. They preside over a court that we try to attend whenever we can, even if we fail to live up to its laws. It is true, is it not, that we long to offer our loyalty to what they represent, but so often fail."

"Of course," my lips moved involuntarily.

"You see, monsieur, the watermark is the invisible poem of my craft. It resides in the paper as a reminder of all the guildsmen that have gone before me. True, it was frequently a fugitive gesture impregnated into paper to carry a subversive message. The image of gnostic amulets that you see here"—M. Poulen indicated a watermark in a sheet of paper in the cabinet below—"were the stock and trade of the Cathars eager to spread their message. The watermark was an act of dissent during the middle ages."

"Are you saying that these watermarks are of an occult nature, that they were the secret language of heresy?"

"The ideas that inspired the Cathars traveled the trade routes from the Middle East. The Cathars were sometimes known as 'weavers,' indicating their association with the cloth industry. Silk merchants from Constantinople regularly sold their goods to the clothiers of the West and so shared their heretical ideas. In this way the dualist beliefs of the Balkan Peninsula, and from as far away as Persia, had managed to enter Europe. It wasn't long before Christianity itself felt threatened."

"Does that make you a heretic as well?" I asked half-jokingly.

"Well, yes, at least insofar as I acknowledge the right of my forbears to hold opposing views to those of their time," replied M. Poulen. "The watermark was their talisman. It allowed them to propagate a belief in the guise of a blank piece of paper. I approve of their ruse. Paper is the most exquisite danger: it offers the illusion of whiteness, of purity, while perpetrating something clandestine."

"It was Marcebru's obsession also."

"You realize now why he was so careful not to write down his poems after Amedée de Jois's death. You see, monsieur, the woman was related to Count Raymond-Roger of Foix. Both his wife, the countess, and his sister Esclarmonde had taken the vows of a Perfect and were considered to be the most holy of women. It is more than likely that Amedée was influenced by her cousin Esclarmonde."

"And so may have become a Perfect herself," I reasoned, referring to the highest spiritual office among the Cathars, the so-called *parfait*. They wore black clothing with a distinctive girdle and leather satchel that invariably contained a copy of the New Testament. Perfects practiced chastity, in contrast to the Elect, or ordinary members of the congregation. The impregnable city of Montségur, the last stronghold of the Cathars, had belonged to Princess Esclarmonde by inheritance. There she had presided over a congress of Perfects. A remarkable woman in her own right, the princess was not averse to debating with Catholic preachers at her brother's court in defense of her faith.

"Perhaps," M. Poulen responded. "All we do know is that Amedée de Jois died at the Abbey Saint-Martin, not far from Foix, under mysterious circumstances. If she had been secretly a heretic, and at the same time a nun, then surely this is reason enough for conflict. It is hard indeed to bear the full burden of one belief; but two? No one should be asked to do so."

M. Poulen's explanation was like that of the watermark itself: in a vague pattern offering only the slightest of clues, he was able to detect subtle meanings and motivations.

If Amedée de Jois had been a Cathar, and perhaps a Perfect, then I could understand Marcebru's secrecy about the nature of her death. People who were known to have held heretical beliefs often found themselves victims of recrimination, with their graves liable to desecration. The Albigensian movement had driven a stake through the heart of

Aquitaine during the twelfth century. The king of France, the pope, and those northern nobles enlisted to their cause finally succeeded in destroying this remarkable, if quixotic uprising at Montségur in 1244, when their fortress was finally destroyed and two hundred Perfects burned to death without trial.

Where did Marcebru stand in this conflict? His sympathies would have surely been with the Cathars, since they, like himself, despised the corrupt clergy and the intervention of Louis VIII and his army on behalf of Rome. His poetry displayed a tough puritan streak toward those who sought patronage from either king or church. The local aristocracy, men like Count Raymond, also sympathized with the Cathars. The troubadours most likely echoed their sympathies, since they were reliant on their patronage.

M. Poulen had alerted me to the possible presence of a hidden side to Marcebru that was governed not only by *fin' amors,* but also by a conflict of allegiances. Amedée de Jois's death may have been linked to dissent in Aquitaine, whether she had wanted it or not. Church and king opposed the provincial aristocracy and the people. Between these forces Marcebru had tried to survive, without aligning himself to either. He had made his poetry a mask for an inner religion in order to protect himself.

Thanking M. Poulen for his help, I stepped into

the square again and wandered over to the Chapel of
Our Lady to pay my respects to the Black Madonna.
Blackened by candle wax, the walnut statue continued
to glow above the altar. All about her votive offerings
testified to her enduring effect on the lives of pilgrims
throughout the centuries. I felt suddenly at ease, without knowing why. As comrades in arms Marcebru and
I knelt before her and offered up our prayers.

Quitting the place, I gazed at the cliff face above
the doorway. I noticed a sword stuck in the stone
halfway up to its hilt. A plaque revealed that it was
none other than Roland's legendary sword of Duran-
dal. Transfixed in stone, this blade had once defended
Europe against the Moor. Yet in spite of Roland's
stand at Roncevalles, he hadn't been able to prevent
that rich current of ideas continuing their invasion
from Spain and the East. Along the trade routes they
had come, transforming everyone they touched. It
was left to individuals to learn how to grapple with
them and make them their own.

Roland, meanwhile, had died defending an impossible dream—a pure and untrammeled Europe
that was resistant to other men's visions. And according to legend, his sword had been transported to Rocamadour by the archangel Michael, far from the
marauding Saracens, at the behest of his dying prayer
in the pass at Roncevalles.

12

A LADY OF
DAMASCUS

THE ROAD from Rocamadour to Figeac crossed a limestone plateau steeped in autumn colors. Even the stones of the region were warmed by a golden light as they vied with the occasional maple tree whose leaves continued to glow throughout the afternoon. On this remote pilgrimage route to Compostela I found myself sharing the memories and tales of those bent upon recollecting their long journey to Spain.

The death roll was my sole companion that morning as I drove along the back roads. It lay on the front seat of the Deux Cheveaux I had hired for the trip, a cylinder of words, all jostling one another as the rear suspension on the vehicle rose and fell. My destination was the church at Caniac-du-Causse, which was built by the monks of Marcilhac-sur-Célé, and the village of Soulomes, whose church had once been a commandery of the Order of the Knights Templars.

Inside the church at Caniac I discovered a crypt dedicated to the relics of Saint Namphaise, an officer in the army of Charlemagne who became a hermit. Marcebru had stopped here on his way north, presumably to gaze upon a number of small lakes said to be carved out of the barren landscape by the saint himself. Under a fluted vault shaded by a colonnade I produced the death roll and read the words of titulis sancti Gafredus, a monk who had resided here:

> "Wars are the relics of dirth. Our warrior-saint knew this when he retired to this place to carve out his sacred lakes. He gave up the Sword in favor of the Word. Death blunted one for him while the other was sharpened by Eternal Life. Marcebru, you are a Warrior of the Word: wield it as Saint Namphaise once did in the service of his king. But *slice through* every hypocrisy that masquerades as truth. As to Amedée de Jois, look upon her as your Whetstone ready to brighten your Blade."

Strong words from a monk living in a desert of carved lakes and stones! Did Marcebru bow his head in self-reproach? Or did he take his leave from the man in a mood of resolve? The reiteration of his need to break with loss must have been galling to him at times. A man can hear others tell him what to do so often before sinking into despondency. Celibates all of them, the monks would never have experienced the sweet lance of sensual love, or indeed *fin' amors* piercing their souls. Their distant love, if they possessed one, had been stored forever in the armory of another world.

In the village of Soulomes I pulled up outside a church whose Romanesque belfry was filled with pigeons. Inside the chancel I discovered a fresco portraying a Knight Templar kneeling at the feet of the Entombed and Resurrected Christ. Here, I suspected, Marcebru's next correspondent must have reverentially laid down his sword and prayed before taking Holy Communion. Carefully I opened the death roll and read:

> "This tongue of *trobar clus* in which you speak, Marcebru, is the language of the gods. I recall once, when we were negotiating a truce with the Caliph of Damascus, we had occasion to stay at his court. Fine foods were served by slaves as we lay on divans listening to an entertainment. The sound of *rehap* and *ney* filled the hallway with such a soulful melody that I felt my heart about to burst. I rose, took my leave, and walked into the courtyard, where a fountain softly splashed.

"There I meditated upon the futility of war. The stars above reminded me of all those souls lost in interminable battles waged in the name of Christ and Allah. Such adversaries! Crescent and Cross had become symbols of a deeper conflict: the desire of men to wound one another with their beliefs. And here I was, attempting to find common ground. Tears came to my eyes, not of happiness but of frustration.

"As if from a mist I sensed someone close by. I turned to see a woman standing by the fountain, her face veiled as is the custom. When I spoke to her she bowed her head, allowing her head cloth to fall away. I recognized a young lady, a princess. I understood every word of her conversation, but to this day I cannot say whether she spoke in Provençal, French, Greek, or Arabic. Her language was as mysterious as her presence.

"'Good knight,' she said. 'You come from a far place where the yearning for origins still flails you like a whip. As dry as this land is, every stone of it is saturated with the spirit we both worship. Naturally we all want to drink at its source, secure in the knowledge that such waters will heal us. And yet we war with one another, scimitar against sword, Koran against Bible, two invincible poems locked in mortal combat.

" 'Is this not the time to tame words in the interest of amity, find a common language so that love might finally erase the disjointure between peoples? Remember that we adore the same essence, which, for all the vaunted subtlety at our disposal, defies expression. We people of Allah, as you know, are seduced by the word. We count the poet as nearer to heaven than the angels.

" 'I entreat you, good knight, return to your people. Say that you have drunk at the fountain of knowledge. When asked what it tasted like, tell them from henceforth your lips tingle with a sensation beyond all other palpable experience. For you have learned to understand the yearning that is rooted in the silence of these stones.'

"At the conclusion of the woman's address I tore my gaze from the fountain to look at her, but she was gone. All that remained of her presence was the scent of lavender. Her apparition had departed as it had come.

"I returned to the hallway, to the music and festivities, my lips aflame. From that day onward I turned my back on Outremer, long home to my most fervent ideals, and sailed back to France. I had discovered that rhetoric is like a eunuch—without gender, it massages the spirit with all the unguents of pleasure, but in truth is no more than the salve of annihilation.

"For this reason, Marcebru, I ask you to consider your own Promised Land. Turn your back on common talk and proceed deeper into the enclosure of the poem. Your task is to ensure that words rise above the task of representing how things are; they must unveil their inner meaning, the language of the gods. This I have heard from a lady in Damascus."

I rolled up the *rouleau de mort,* oblivious to the steady gaze of Christ Resurrected above the altar. I felt the flame of the Knight Templar's words. The death roll had become a living torch, despite having remained untended in the Chapelle des Pénitents all those centuries, starved of the kindling of thought. For it demanded of me as much as of Marcebru to take up the staff and begin the pilgrimage along the path toward knowledge.

The Knight Templar's remarks were still as powerful and alive as the day they were written. His conversation with Marcebru had touched on themes that nonetheless went beyond the merely personal. The veiled visitor at the fountain had cast her spell over two men—and now, eight hundred years later, was reasserting her claim over consciousness. I had become the third man as eager as they to plumb the mystery of her words.

The fresco above my head shimmered. The scene of the Entombment continued to reaffirm the transience of death, while in contrast, the Resurrection called upon people to stand up, to resist. The Templar, meanwhile, old sword bearer that he was, had finally hung up his sword. And his friend the poet, whose song was temporarily in abeyance, was listening to some other tune—of lavender and the sweet scent of words.

———

13

THE BASALT TABLET

IN MY ATTEMPT to understand Marcebru I felt myself slipping back in time. His relationship with Amedée de Jois had become my obsession. She, a dualist's cousin, had taken vows in order to escape an extreme predicament. Aquitaine was in crisis—people didn't know which doctrine to believe in, and the world beyond its frontiers was threatened. Where could an individual escape except into a private act of meditation?

Fin' amors was just such an escape. It offered an opportunity to love someone at a distance, without reciprocity, demanding only that this person should bear silent witness to one's love. Marcebru, however, had begun to distrust the idea of *fin' amors,* believing it had become sullied by faithlessness. If love were to transform him, then it must enjoy absolute fidelity. It may be that Amedée de Jois found the burden of this ideal too great.

In Figeac, where I planned to stay the night, Marcebru had encountered Père Fyot, the abbot of Saint-Sauveur Abbey. Judging by the few remarks in the death roll that had survived, the two men may well have discussed a range of interesting topics, perhaps late into the evening. The writing on the original document had been illegible in places, prompting the Latin scholar in Ussel to remark (in parentheses) that he thought wine must have been spilled on the parchment. All he had been able to translate were a few enigmatic fragments:

> . . . fantasy may err in the particular . . .
> and images slacken the exercise of the Cross.
> A fruitful garden springs from . . . ground
> . . . stillness . . .
> . . . inner eye seeks . . .
> . . . hot perfumes of Paradise.
> Thought is an instrument secretly dispersed . . .
> . . . End returns to its origin . . .
> Divine . . . a treasure hidden among burrs . . . Grasp the nettle and feel the pain of meaning as it draws blood . . .
> . . . sting of an asp.

Amedée de Jois understood . . .

. . . .

. . . nothing terrible in not living.

How Marcebru and Abbé Fyot must have talked. Whatever the good abbé had said, to the most cursory examination his remarks indicated him to have been a learned man. His final remark, addressed to the memory of Amedée de Jois, suggested that he had studied his Epicurus well, as I knew these words by heart.

The more I studied the death roll, the more I regarded it as an inspired document. Though many of the correspondents drew upon the Bible to make their point, most were encouraged by their encounter with Marcebru to be more adventurous. The death he wished to commemorate had acted as a catalyst, provoking a renewed emphasis upon individual thought. Obviously these people were challenged by their own attempts to discourage Marcebru from continuing his prolonged dalliance with remorse.

As well as being Abbé Fyot's home, Figeac was also the residence of a forgotten language. My guidebook informed me that a replica of the Rosetta Stone, sculpted in black granite from Zimbabwe by an American in 1990, lay in the courtyard of the Place des Escritures, surrounded by a group of medieval buildings. It was here that the great orientalist Jean-François

Champollion was born in 1790, and where he dedicated his life to deciphering the Egyptian hieroglyphs. In a museum housing a replica from the Rosetta Stone on the square, other documents pertaining to Champollion's work could be viewed, including a canopic vase bearing human entrails, a scribe's palette considered to be an essential item of mortuary equipment, and a mummy's costume decoration.

I couldn't help being reminded of Abbé Fyot's fragmentary remarks in the death roll when I thought of the painstaking research conducted by Champollion. Both men had been obsessed with expression and the reluctance of phrases to reveal their original meaning. I decided that a visit to the museum was in order. Champollion might ease the frustration I felt in the wake of Marcebru's silence.

No one was about when I entered the arched gateway to the Place des Escritures. Imbedded in the cobbles lay a huge piece of black granite nearly fifty feet long and half as much wide, with the characters from the Rosetta Stone chiseled in its surface. I all but tripped over one of its protruding edges as I entered the courtyard. There! I thought. I've stumbled over the meaning of words throughout my life, and now I've managed to do so physically as well. Feeling rather stupid, I brushed my shoe on the back of my trousers.

"I must have that edge attended to." A man's voice addressed me from a doorway at the end of the courtyard. He wore a beret, a scarf loosely draped around his neck, and a blue polo shirt. His smoothly shaven face had a slightly waxy look.

"I wasn't looking where I was going," I replied.

"The same could be said for all of us. Immersed as we are in our own thoughts sometimes, we often fail to recognize where they are taking us simply because we ignore their signs."

I was nonplussed by this remark and said so.

"Ah, monsieur, please excuse me. Let me introduce myself. I am the concierge of this museum. I live within the domain of the word throughout the summer season." He gave a short laugh, its brevity more noticeable than its actual sound. "Imagine overseeing a huge black stone written in three extinct languages, each one as untranslatable as the next. I ask myself sometimes how M. Champollion survived his ordeal, patiently unraveling every hieroglyph and matching it against these parallel texts we see here. 'Symbolic versus phonetic,' he used to mutter. Which precedes the other, thought or word? The hen or the egg, I say. It is a question none of us can answer, and so the mystery remains."

"Do we know what the Stone says?" I asked.

"It is a state edict written at the time of the

Ptolemies, who reigned between 332 and 80 BCE.
Much of it is to do with the security of temples and
the grain tax awarded to each. One might call it an
early example of commercial language. There is
nothing here that suggests magical invocation or
prayers to the dead."

"The language of the gods, you mean."

"Unless a god's share of vines and fruit trees can
be interpreted to mean as much."

"Monsieur," I said. "Perhaps you can help me."

I went on to explain to the man my interest in
Marcebru and his death roll. I felt the need to unbur-
den myself, and the concierge's manner made me suspect that I had met someone of like mind. He watched
over words that had lost their meaning; while I tried to
revive their meaning before it was too late.

"A poet's silence is a complex issue," the
concierge replied. "He may be responding to stimuli
beyond the range of ordinary people. Poetry is important to the world, not just because it gives expression to it, but also in the way it renews the world. It
changes us as ordinary thinking cannot."

"This may well be why Champollion was inspired to translate the Rosetta Stone," I proposed.
"He may have suspected that this new path lay in the
symbolic images discarded by an ancient culture.
The hieroglyph, after all, is a potent picture."

"Where the Stone says, for example, 'these gods-who-love-their-father undertake much in the service of the temples of Egypt,' we sense the continuing power of incantation. Today we no longer acknowledge the power of language in this way."

"Marcebru also experienced such a loss, and so fell silent," I replied. "Once the power of *fin' amors* had waned, his ability to sing died with it. For him, it appears *fin' amors* found its object in Amedée de Jois. When she died, so too did his ability to create."

"From what you have told me, Marcebru's ability to sing was linked to an ideal. So long as he worshipped Amedée de Jois he was able to celebrate the spirit of distant love. But when she died—ah, we know what happened to Jaufré Rudel and the countess of Tripoli. His death prompted her to take the veil, you might recall. Her life changed as soon as she accepted Rudel's death as an expression of his love. Love and death became entangled as light and gravity are intertwined."

"Your argument is hard to follow," I was forced to admit.

"Normally we regard gravity and light as mutually exclusive. They are not, really. Gravity is the act of weighing down, of withdrawing from airiness. Light, on the other hand, clears and reveals the path toward airiness. They are bound to one another, concealment and revelation, obscurity and openness, darkness and illumination. This is the principle underlying *fin' amors*—gravity and light are inclusive rather than opposed to one another."

"You are saying that love and death are inseparable."

"We have been laboring for too long under a mistaken belief that in love or in death we grow apart," replied the concierge. "For the ancient Egyptians, making the crossover from life into death was a poetic act, not something merely physical. Remember the *Book of the Dead,* and those endless hieroglyphics on the walls in the Pharoahs' tombs? The body, you see, could be transported into the afterlife only on a chariot of words. This is why a scribe's palette was always placed among the funeral equipment: it helped the deceased transcribe his journey to the underworld."

The concierge's portrayal of love and death prompted me to reconsider Marcebru's silence in the wake of Amedée's death. His silence was affirmative, a tribute to her, rather than merely being elegiac. In the same way, the black basalt tablet in the courtyard, which had concealed for so long the secrets of language, had finally joined forces with Champollion's insight. Between them they had revealed the possibility of an unbroken relationship with the world.

Taking dinner alone that evening in a local café, and ruminating over a glass of Armagnac while the table was being cleared away, I decided to return to Place des Escritures for one more look at the Rosetta Stone. Befuddlement probably affected my state of mind, but I was sober enough to recall the route back to the courtyard. An evening chill sharpened my senses, and I noticed how luminous the night seemed.

The square was in darkness, except for the pale light of the moon. I made my way to the center of the Rosetta Stone, aware that I was stepping into a quarry of words. Blackness surrounded me, and the letters of three ancient languages beneath me seemed to cause my feet to tingle. The hieroglyphs began to converge on me then, and I wanted to break free somehow. I wanted, at least once, to disassociate myself from the meaning of words. But remembering one of Abbé Fyot's remarks, I realized this was impossible: the inner eye *is* always longing to discover the hot perfume of paradise.

The taste of Armagnac still on my lips, I asked myself whether Marcebru may have turned his back on the word. Perhaps he had sought death in the piercing light of its absence. Whatever had occurred all those years ago, he had left me with this as yet unsolved riddle.

14

BORN OF TWO DESIRES

WHERE WAS THIS JOURNEY leading? Laden down as I was by the weight of the death roll I had become a beast of burden, carrying about what others had tossed aside. It had begun to weigh me down: I longed to free myself from this pilgrimage of concealment and revelation. There, gravity again! The concierge who cared for the replica of the Rosetta Stone was also right: I refused to admit how weightiness and revelation might be allies.

Were these values not also those of Marcebru when he contrasted the fragmented way (*frait*) with integrated thinking (*entiers*)? Certainly he strove to achieve a high moral tone in his poetry. Colors, objects, trees, plants, animals, insects, birds—all of these he used as symbols to conceal rather than reveal. This was the essence of the "closed style" for which he was known.

His songs were like hieroglyphs. Rereading one of his poems that I carried about in my backpack, it was evident that he saw nature casting a net over the receptive mind:

> The leaf twists as I see it fall
> From the treetops, and the wind
> Tears it apart in its giddy descent,
> So I value the bitterness of winter
> More than a summer full of hot resources
> Which is a parent to wantonness
> And the comeliness of desire.
>
> Woodpecker and nightingale
> Turn their song into silence,
> As do jay and oriole, in the
> Wake of winter's pleasure;
> While summer's pride bares
> Its fangs in the face of ruffians
> As they knock it down
> In a gutter full of complaints.

Winter is a chaste season. It draws pleasure from the birds that it silences—those birds whose harsh calls and bright feathers are a reflection of empty talk and shallow summer love. Pride, with its savage summer smile, is also tossed aside by winter's complaints. Arrogance, temptation, and annoyance are swept away by nature.

Marcebru's death roll was a celebration of darkness, of secrecy, of the shadowy side of Amedée de Jois. Whoever she was, this woman had provided Marcebru with a new sense of himself. In quitting life she chose to transform his conception of love. Such a gesture wasn't so unreasonable if she had, in fact, discovered for herself what lay beyond *fin' amor.* Marcebru indicated as much in a poem that suggests that she was not of this world—that love "born of two desires" was more precious to her than life itself:

> That pair of lovers, so suited,
> Who do not oppose one another
> In their voyage, with love
> At their side, are clear proof
> Of one wish born of two desires
> And trust that is secure, white,
> Precious, true and pure.

Had I failed to recognize something important in my investigation of Marcebru—namely, that a particular quality of love was an intrinsic part of the death roll? Knowing that our modern idea of love is tinged with emotion, I had to be careful not to project such views onto those of Marcebru and his age.

Alone among poets, he had attempted to define *fin'
amors* as a philosophic value in one of his poems:

> He who is chosen by *fin' amors*
> Lives a happy life, courtly and wise,
> While he whom it rejects, it refutes
> And condemns to destruction.
> If a man disdains *fin' amors*
> He becomes a fool, gawping
> At illusion and totally misled
> By the stupidity of his thinking.

A clear mind and praiseworthy conduct were
more appropriate to love than mere physical excite-
ment. The death roll, whose theme lay in remembering Amedée de Jois, was deeply imbued with ideas
that rose above the personal. Marcebru had asked
everyone he met to write down their thoughts in the
hope that they might engender new insights.

Already partway through my journey, I felt that I
was traveling toward something as yet unexpressed. A
woman's death and a poet's silence conscribed all my
actions. I had become enmeshed in their solitude and
could no longer escape the demands they had made
upon one another, nor those who had been called
upon to contribute to the death roll.

———

15

CONFLICTS AND
RELIQUARIES

—

Albi is the only town in Europe whose name is
directly linked to heresy. The Church dubbed the dualist Cathar doctrine the "Albigensian heresy" at the beginning of the thirteenth century, thus bringing upon
this rose-colored city the condemnation of the past. It
may be that Albi embodied a passive spirit of political,
social, and spiritual anarchy that made the rest of Europe feel uneasy. As in other cities in Aquitaine, a
mosque, a synagogue, a place of heretical worship, and
a Christian church could exist there side by side.

This pluralism made it possible for a Moorish
professor and a Jewish court official to engage in civi-
lized conversation. Women such as the Perfect Esclarmonde were free to attend court and debate theology
with inquisitors from the north and not feel de-
meaned. This sophisticated and worldly society had

refined sexuality to the point where chastity (*castitatz*) meant more than physical abstention. It now embraced the control and ordering of sexual desire.

Such sweet pain was derived from the Arab poets of Spain, men like Ibn Hazm and Ibn Dā'ūd, who propounded the concept of profane love in the early eleventh century. The practice of a chaste love (*al-hawa al-'udri*), implying renunciation, was considered to be a sign of a man's good character. The troubadour Guilhem de Montanhagol, who fought in Spain and who was deeply influenced by Moorish poets, wrote that love sprang from chastity rather than passion. To Guilhem, a lady was fashioned by God:

> I am persuaded and convinced
> That from Heaven her beauty came,
> The creation of Paradise does she seem
> And her grace barely of this world.

This idea was later taken up by Andreas Capellanus in his treatise *De amore,* written in 1186 at the behest of Marie de Champagne. *Amor purus,* he wrote, in contrast to *amor mixtus,* "consists in the contemplation of the mind and affection of the heart; it goes as far as the kiss and the embrace and the modest contact with the nude lover. . . . This love is distinguished by being of such virtue that from it arises all excellence of character, and no injury comes from it, and God sees very little offense in it. No maiden can ever be corrupted by such a love, nor can a widow or wife receive any harm or suffer any injury to her reputation."

The nobles of Albi nurtured a belief in humankind's capacity to seek and find happiness. The tension between the sensual and the spiritual, which poets such as Marcebru and Montanhagol attempted to resolve in their work, finally succumbed to the Christian rejection of the carnal. When this occurred *fin' amors* was consumed by inquisitorial fires and the armies of Simon de Montfort wreaking havoc with the sword.

Was Albi the sane man and the rest of France the town gone mad that the poet Piere Cardinal was alluding to in his famous fable?

There is a certain town, I know not where, upon which rain fell of such a nature that all the inhabitants upon whom it fell lost their reason. All lost their reason except one, who escaped because he was asleep in his house when the rains came. When he awoke, he rose: the rain had ceased, and he went out among the people who were committing follies. One was clothed, another naked, another was spitting at the sky: some were throwing sticks and stones, tearing their coats, striking and pushing. . . . The sane man was deeply surprised and saw that they were mad; nor could he find a single man in his senses. Yet greater was their surprise at him, and as they saw that he did not follow their example, they concluded that he had lost his senses. . . . so one strikes him in front, another behind; he is dashed to the ground and trampled underfoot. . . . At length he flees to his house covered with mud, bruised and half dead, and thankful for his escape.

Marcebru must have felt like the only sane man left in the world when he entered Albi with the death roll over his shoulder. The greatest conflict of his age could be reduced to a single premise: Did evil, as the Cathars believed, exist in its own right? Or was it no more than a drifting away from good, a most devious illusion, as theologians since Augustine so fervently preached? Either way, Aquitaine was torn apart by those who rejected one or other of these views. Living with paradox as he did, Marcebru had chosen not to give up his life to defend something so clearly insoluble.

Like a hooded *capucié* or member of a secret society known as the Brothers of Peace, who roamed the countryside in an attempt to stamp out brigandage, he traveled the back roads of Aquitaine seeking to root out all crudity of expression, his only weapon the subtle art of poetry. It was enough for him to know that some men, secretly, longed to test their mettle against his ardency.

"In our beloved priory," a monk from Abbey Saint-Foy of Conques wrote, "there exists a small statue of our saint. He is constructed of many parts—a head from Rome, arms from the time of Charlemagne, and a torso from the time of Clovis, King of the Franks. It is adorned with enamels, cabochons, and precious stones from a more recent period. This sacred reliquary partakes of all ages, spanning time, overcoming even Our Lord's anguish with its intaglio and engraved crystal. Just so, Marcebru, poet of powers, in whom all engravure is a sin, allow disjointedness to overcome your grief."

———

"Yes, and more," wrote the lay brother Giraldo, who had read the previous epistle. "We also possess the initial 'A' given to the abbey by Charlemagne himself. It is a piece of the True Cross upon which Our Lord was crucified, and is contained in a reliquary decorated in chased and gilded silver. 'Alpha' is the first letter of the alphabet, and a signal to us all of the power of the Word. You, Marcebru, are also a reliquary of the Word. Alpha and Omega, the first and the last, only these are you able to resolve. The good Amedée's death is not the end. Pledge yourself to the 'A,' to the beginning as well as the end. There you will discover humanity's gain."

The abbot Hincmar of Saint-Foy penned the following lines of verse:

> None understand what depths
> To which the mind must plunge
> Before it is displaced. The insane
> Cosset a life without contrast; so
> Wrench from their faces that mask
> Of paradox which conceals all
> Mystery, all sage and limpid conflict.
> Erase expression from your gaze:
> Sink back into that bottomless pool
> From which Will stirs and then rises.

Thus did I enter Albi. The death roll had become like a cart in spring, decked out in flowers that were the garlands of men enthralled by the beauty and possibility of words.

16

WHITE FRIENDSHIP

I FELT UNWELL when I booked into my hotel overlooking the Tarn River in Albi. Lunch had been light that day, and there was no reason to assume my illness was caused by something I may have eaten. Determined to shrug it off, I sat by the window and watched the sun warming the cathedral walls on the far side of the river. Saint-Cécile, it seemed, was as flushed as I.

This was a city of deep and painful memories. Its favorite sons were the seafarer Jean-François de Lapéruse, who sailed the Pacific in the 1780s, and the artist Henri Toulouse-Lautrec. Both these men met with early deaths. Knowing that its history was so firmly linked to Catharism, to public burnings and to wars, made me consider whether some cities are blighted by their best endeavors. I knew that Saint-

Cécile had been built with the intention of coming to terms with the anguish of the past.

Imbedded in the stones of Albi was a question. "Whence came evil, and in what does it exist?" wrote Tertullian, invoking the age-old conundrum of existence. Countless residents of this city had asked themselves the same question and resolved it in their own way. Evil existed, and the world was the devil's domain. Man as a physical being was condemned to remain in the world, whereas his soul, if it could disentangle itself from the physical, might ascend to the celestial world. Good and evil were spirits locked in mortal combat within the body.

Man had a simple choice: to purify himself or condemn his soul to an earthbound existence until it had broken free. This act of metempsychosis, where the migration of the soul from one body to another occurs throughout time, finally ended with its release into the celestial world by an act of penance. To indulge in sexual activity, therefore, was to prolong a troubled relationship with the earth. To be chaste aided the spirit in its journey to the celestial world. Acknowledging that Satan did exist made it possible then to understand the enemy—an issue that was lost among those who opposed the Cathars.

Gnosis was as old as the Orient. That it had

somehow attached itself to Christianity, and was worming its way into the very heart of Christian belief, was not lost on Rome. Men such as Saint Dominic argued against the pernicious effects of gnostic thinking, forgetting perhaps that one of its favorite sons, Saint Augustine, had once confessed to being a Manichee. Dualism, as far as the Catholic church was concerned, was more destructive than the plague.

Still unwell, I decided to consult a physician. The hotel reception kindly gave me an address of a doctor nearby, and then called a taxi. I crossed the Old Bridge over the Tarn and made my way through the back streets to an address behind the cloister of Saint-Salvy. I found the doctor's rooms and sat down to wait for my consultation.

"Ah, monsieur, do come in," invited the doctor, a gentleman in his mid-fifties with well-manicured fingernails. His head, though large and somewhat cumbersome in appearance, still managed to give off an air of thoughtfulness and restraint.

The surgery was decorated in ornate wood and was medieval in appearance. Engravings hung on the walls, portraying typical Albian scenes. My eye took them in, pausing only when I noticed a figure of a woman tied to a stake in the middle of a funeral pyre. Obviously this woman had been a Cathar, a Perfect perhaps, who had been condemned to death. At the sight of her suffering, whatever ailed me momentarily departed.

"A blight on our history," the doctor observed, noticing my interest in his engravings. "We live within the shadow of this holocaust, even today."

I made no reply, content to allow the doctor to examine me without interruption. He listened to my chest, prodded my stomach, and felt my pulse. After a few questions as to my reasons for being in Aquitaine, to which I gave him a detailed reply, he finally pronounced his opinion.

"Monsieur," he said. "You are a foreigner venturing into a land of tragedy. We who live here are familiar with the effects of the past. We are immunized against its symptoms. You, on the other hand, have no resistance."

"I presume there is nothing organically wrong with me," I replied.

"The past can be a mental condition, monsieur. When it is filled with suffering, with anguish, and with other conditions of the heart, so will it affect your general health. Your encounter with Marcebru, and with the death of his *fin' amors,* has affected you more than you realize. I do not mean this in a psychological sense, not at all. That would be too superficial a prognosis. The subject of belief—or shall I say, this conflict within belief—may have stimulated in you a daring encounter with doubt. I do not say this lightly.

"Dualism is a toxic potion," he continued. "It fired generations of men and women with an instinct for perfection, but at a considerable cost. Our land was ravaged by intolerance, which dealt a mortal blow to the Cathars. They died for believing too fervently in escaping the limitations of their bodies."

"You have an idea, then, how Amedée de Jois may have met her death," I ventured, feeling my illness beginning to recede.

"Amedée de Jois was the cousin of Esclarmonde, one of Aquitaine's most famous Perfects. She had come under her influence. Have you ever heard of the ceremony known as *endura*?" the doctor inquired.

"No," I admitted.

"It was practiced by Perfects who wished to quit life and so reach the celestial kingdom without becoming entangled in matter again. *Endura* is an act of suicide, more often than not by starvation. It was the final expression of Cathar doctrine: the body was destroyed that a soul might be released."

"But we know that Amedée de Jois died a nun in Saint-Martin. So far as I'm aware, she never held Cathar beliefs."

"It is true, she died in the habit of a religious. But there is a tradition that says that under her habit at death they found a distinctive girdle normally worn by a Perfect."

"What are you suggesting?"

"I am imputing nothing, monsieur. I merely wish to point out that in Amedée de Jois the entire conflict of our tiny nation may well have been enacted. Her belief in God, in the Christian sense, was pitted against her desire for perfection. A futile ambition, and one that has plagued we people of Oc since these gnostic ideas first entered our territory along the trade routes from the East."

"Doctors were partly to blame for its dispersal," I reminded him.

"As you say, members of my profession were apologists for dualist beliefs. They were known to have proselytized in many a noble's household. However, they were more leech bearers than doctors as we know them today. They possessed the ability to suck from people what most sustained them."

"Their beliefs, of course."

"No, no. What kept them alive."

We both laughed.

My thoughts returned to the circumstances surrounding Amedée de Jois's death. If she had been a nun, and had also participated in the heretical ceremony known as *endura,* then what could have possibly driven her into such an impasse?

I knew this question must be resolved if I were to understand Marcebru's silence. Obviously he had been aware of the contrasts in her nature. Even if the doctor's assessment were incorrect, it was not hard to imagine her succumbing to the religious controversy of her time. She may well have desired to attain perfection in this life and, paradoxically, knew of no other way to attain it except by dying.

The choice may have been far simpler. Amedée de Jois may have died because she no longer believed in the power of the word to express her deepest desires. Controversy and argument, theological disputation and heretical diatribe, all these made it difficult to discern the truth. Far from making things clear for her, words may have created a moat of misunderstanding rather than a bridge.

Was it love that she had yearned for and lost? She, the object of *fin' amors,* may have finally succumbed to a loss of passion. The Cathar doctrine of disenchantment with the physical may have destroyed her relationship with her own body and so destroyed her love for Marcebru. Moreover, her feelings for Marcebru may have fallen victim to her desire to attain perfection.

"Since you are my last patient for the day," the doctor's voice interrupted my thoughts, "let's take a stroll through the cloister of Saint-Salvy. After the fatigue of work I often sit in its gardens and allow its stones to speak."

I assented, and together we walked along the cobbled lanes toward the cloister. My illness had completely departed and I felt my old self again.

"I want to show you something," the doctor remarked as we entered the cloister. A few people sat around, reading newspapers or gazing at the ruined capitals. The doctor indicated two sculpted figures on one of the capitals—a man and a woman, arms about one another in a formal embrace. "I tell myself that these figures represent Marcebru, the poet, and his *fin' amors,* Amedée de Jois," he added.

"Their faces appear to have been erased," I said, noting the smoothness of their visages. "How can you identify them?"

"As a doctor I am accustomed to diagnosing illness. My task is to probe below the surface. These sculptures have not revealed their identity because there are few who are prepared to imagine who they are. You see, monsieur, and I include you in my assessment, some of us are dedicated to the task of imagining what is not there. We choose to invest in their absence something of ourselves. Thus we are capable of distancing ourselves from who we are, like Marcebru and Amedée de Jois. They chose to listen to the voice that whispered their destiny more than they did their desires."

"They made a pact?"

"In a sense, yes."

"Of white friendship," I managed to say, recalling some words I had read in one of Marcebru's poems.

"White friendship?" The doctor raised his eyebrows. "I have never heard such an expression."

I recited some lines in the original Provençal from Marcebru's poem:

> *Non puosc dompnas trobar gair*
> *Que blanch' armistatz no.i vaire*
> *A presen o a saubuda*
> *N'aja vergoigna perduda*
> *Si que la meins afrontada*
> *N'a laissat cazer un caire.*

> Rarely do I find ladies in whom
> White friendship has not sullied,
> Or all sense of modesty been lost
> Secretly or otherwise. Or that
> The least brazen of them
> Hasn't let her veil fall from it.

"Remarkable," the doctor observed. "White friendship may well have been their ideal, and of course the reason for their pact. Not even in death could they be parted."

I gazed up at the carved relief of the faceless lovers. They seemed so composed. The absence of any expression, however, could not erase my feeling of sympathy for their predicament. Intimacy was their emblem as they struggled to come to terms with what was their most heartfelt estrangement. Their very separation bound them to one another more completely than if they had been together, lovers to whom death was no more than a distant prospect.

"Monsieur *le docteur*," I responded. "I must thank you for your clinical advice. It seems that whatever ailed me earlier has disappeared. I feel like a new man."

"That, my friend, is entirely problematic, for any of us. Even the Cathars learned to their cost that perfection can be an illusory condition—almost, may I say, an illness."

Above us, the lovers barely touched one another as they embraced. For the first time I began to imagine a certain physical presence in their gazes. In Amedée de Jois I saw fine cheekbones—yes, and eyes in which the world glowed. On Marcebru's forehead, however, I noted only wounds.

———

17

AMONG THE RUINS

THE FURTHER I VENTURED into the old land of Oc, the more I realized how the journey was changing me. Of course, discovering why Marcebru tossed the death roll into the river remained uppermost in my mind. But it had also become a personal quest whereby I became conscious of my own relationship with the facts as they began to reveal themselves. Aquitaine had become a land of questions—as much for me as they were for Marcebru.

The concepts of love, death, good, evil, all these converged. No words could possibly express what they really meant. Those who defended perfection, and those who condemned it as heresy, were trying to find words to say what couldn't be said. The doctor was right: truth was an illness. Marcebru and I were a part of the same conflict: whether to abandon this journey of recovery, or press onward?

I was traveling through an ancient and unresolved quandary, while the wanderings of a grief-stricken poet had begun to reflect a people who were out of step with life. Opposing beliefs had inflamed people to scale new heights and to embark on new endeavors. Tragically, for Aquitaine, the old order had triumphed.

Simon de Montfort fought a prolonged and bitter campaign against the Cathars during the early years of the thirteenth century. He took no prisoners. The death by burning of so many Perfects, the destruction of towns and villages, the hounding of men into exile in Lombardy and faraway Bulgaria, led not only to the destruction of the land of Oc, but also to the desecration of that *joie* so essential to its soul.

During his lifetime Marcebru had sung the praises of *joie* from the court of Castile to the drawing rooms of Guyenne, celebrating it wherever he went. His was a journey of inner assent as he tramped the byways of poetry in search of its essence. At the heart of his search, it seems, was his belief in *joie* as an act of life enrichment rather than the expression of any pious endeavor generated by formal belief or dogma.

Nor was his journey through Aquitaine with the death roll any different. At Guilhem-le-Désert, a monastery built at the mouth of two untamed river gorges, a piece of the True Cross found in the church there had obviously influenced the remarks made by its abbot, Foulques.

The monastery's patron, Guilhem, the grandson of Charles Martel and childhood friend of Charlemagne, later became one of the emperor's ablest officers. He won numerous battles at Nîmes, Orange, and Narbonne before defeating the Saracens at Barcelona. On his return to France, and hearing of the death of his much-loved wife, he decided to dedicate himself to a life of solitude.

Charlemagne made a gift of the piece of the True Cross to his great friend for his loyalty and support. Guilhem eventually retired to the Gellone Valley, where he built his monastery. He died there in 812 in the "odor of sanctity," as the chronicles relate.

In the death roll Abbé Folques wrote:

> "Our abbey was built by a warrior saint, one Saint Guilhem. It was he who put up his sword in favor of the Word. Defense of the True Cross and all that it represents is part of our belief. Solitude, and the clear waters of these gorges, are the armor we need to ward off the devil. He lurks under habits and in the cavernous maw of heresy. Men must embrace the True Faith if they are to resist the

armies of the infidel, masquerading as they do in the words of the *cathari*.

"Marcebru, the death of your beloved is tainted. It is Calvary's nails, piercing your flesh with the hard ecstasy of regret. Your Descent is imminent: allow your body to be bathed in myrrh whose perfume is so redolent of honey and roses. We at Saint-Guilhem wish you well."

Beatie Marie, the abbess of the convent of Saint-Enimie, built among the ancient stone terraces of the Tarn Gorge, where vines, almonds, walnut, cherry, and peach trees are still cultivated, wrote sentiments that may have also been derived from the memory of the founder of her house.

Saint Enimie, it seems, was a Merovingian princess who rejected all proposals of marriage, preferring to dedicate herself to God. Her father, the king, nonetheless betrothed her to one of his barons. The young woman promptly fell ill with leprosy, and her suitor abandoned her. One day, in a dream, an angel ordered Enimie to leave for Gévaudan, where a spring would restore her to her previous beauty. At the Source de Burie she dived in and was miraculously cured. No sooner had she left the valley, however, than the symptoms of her disease returned. Seeing this as a sign from God, Enimie decided to retire to a cave and live a solitary life. She died in 628 and is buried in a fine silver reliquary, which has become an object of pilgrimage. Many miracles are associated with her name.

In the death roll Beatie Marie wrote:

"We praise her memory, she who renounced love for Love. No reliquary is bright enough to bear her precious bones. The gates to the ossuary of anguish have swung wide to receive her. We who remain in this life, the simple souls in whom sin cavorts like squirrels in spring—we attend lauds in her honor. We remember that she, cousin to the archpriest of heresy, renounced All rather than compromise her loyalty to the living or the dead.

"Poet, wanderer between worlds, consider her death as a gift. In Amedée de Jois martyrdom lies like a holy diadem upon the heads of us all."

Or Etienne de Muret, the founder of the priory of Comberoumal, an austere hermit who had renounced his worldly goods and retired to the solitude of the mountains. Here he had built a small cloister, sober in design, and a church with windows above the nave. Light was said to flow through those windows like the wings of angels.

He wrote:

> In faraway Egypt in a cave
> Anthony showed us the way.
> Ravens fed him and desert lions
> He tamed, sure of bounty
> Under the auspices of solitude.
> With their barbed tails, devils
> Stabbed him until he bled
> Tears of praise in the name
> Of Our Savior, one Christus,
> Whose Crown of Thorns
> Scars our brow to this day.

> That maid has heard His call
> And surrendered to His shrouds.
> Death in the habit of darkness
> Was small comfort in the wake
> Of her battle with the devil.
> It's said white friendship
> Was her calling; I say
> A river of lust consumed her
> With its torrent.

Praise and blame accompanied the memory of Amedée de Jois wherever Marcebru went. Realizing that this confusion surrounding the mystery of her death had rubbed off on me, I found myself alone one late autumn day standing in the ruined fortress of Minerve, surrounded by a region of arid gorges. Below, the Cesse and Briant rivers converged. Prehistoric caves littered the steep riverbank, and leaves crowded the pathway among the broken battlements.

It was here, in 1210, that one of the most dramatic battles of the Albigensian Crusade occurred. Simon de Montfort, at the head of seven thousand men, made his stand at the gates to this fortress. Inside, numerous Cathars sought refuge. After five weeks of siege and running low on water, the townspeople finally surrendered. Montfort offered them a choice: recant and be converted, or be put to the sword. On that day one hundred and eighty Perfects offered themselves as martyrs to their cause.

Amedée de Jois had chosen the same path. She had sought death rather than suffer the ignominy of failing in her quest. The tall pine trees nearby, their sturdy trunks rising above the ruined walls, were reminiscent of aspiration and her dream of the perfect life. It may have also been the symptom of her loss.

Leaning on the battlements overlooking the rivers, I tried to understand what had pressed Amedée de

Jois and Marcebru toward the attainment of this elusive white friendship. What had Marcebru hoped to gain? Was their love flawed in some way? I began to think that each of them harbored a secret that neither was prepared to reveal to the other.

A female tourist approached me as I leaned against the battlement, perhaps misjudging my mood.

"Monsieur," she inquired. "I sincerely hope you are feeling all right."

"Of course. I was merely thinking about all those Perfects who died here in defense of their beliefs," I said. "It seems such a tragedy."

"So many good men and women martyred," the woman commiserated. "What hatred was unleashed. If Montfort had cared more about life than he did religious orthodoxy, this would never have happened."

"We must never forget that," I replied.

I tried to imagine Marcebru, the death roll over his shoulder, a pilgrim among these thorny issues, pricked and bleeding.

"Life is its own gift, not how we choose to order it," the woman observed, plucking a pine cone from one of the trees and tossing it into the gorge.

——

18

THE COURT
OF THE INQUISITOR

—

CARCASSONNE, this city of towers and inquisitorial fires on the banks of the Aude! Marcebru had stayed some days inside its walls, a guest of heretics and the uneasy papal legates eager to expel them before they poisoned the whole of France. He, a poet of freedom and the ennobling power of love, must have regarded himself a stranger in a town later to fall victim to Montfort's army in 1209, and so become one of the most notorious courts of the inquisitor in southern France.

Passing through the redoubt known as Porte Narbonnaise, I entered the city, Marcebru's words lingering in my thoughts. As his shield they protected him against enemy arrows:

Qui ses bauzia
Vol Amor albergar,
De Cortesia
Deu sa maion jonchar;
Get fors feunia
E fol sobreparler;
Pretz e donar
Deu aver en bailia,
Ses ochaio.

Without deceit
He who wishes
To harbor love
Must decorate his house
With courtliness;
Let him throw out
Bad language
And unworthiness;
Without question
He must be a victim
Of generosity and honor.

I hoped his words would be enough to protect me during my stay in Carcassonne. Try as I might, I couldn't dispel the feeling that I was being watched by the ghosts of the inquisitors as they attempted to implicate me. Nor had I any desire to be branded an *agent provocateur.*

I suspected that Marcebru had visited Carcassonne for a reason. Perhaps he had wanted to find out more about Amedée de Jois's links with the Cathar heresy. The Cathar belt discovered under her habit when she died may have provoked in him lingering doubts about her vocation. Was she Catholic or Cathar? In his eyes Amedée de Jois embodied *cortezia,* that quality of perfection he loathed to see annulled, whatever form her belief might have taken.

All I had was the death roll to account for Marcebru's movements. Like a reliquary it contained the gnarled fingers of language, each word in concert with opinion, with mystery, and with prejudice. I had become its guardian, its keeper. No more was I carrying about a translation of some water-stained parchment, but a text of revelation.

Installed in a small hotel off Place Saint-Jean, I took out the death roll and read the remarks of some of those people Marcebru had met in Carcassonne:

> "You ask for some particular patchwork to be sewn onto your soul," wrote Raymonde Arsen, an illiterate tailor who had allowed her words to be transcribed by Marcebru. "But we humble folk only know how to

shape from oblivion our fallen nature. It is all we have!"

━━━

"I have been an ass and a squirrel in different lives," confessed Pierre Clergue, a shepherd arrested for heresy who wore a yellow cross on his coat as part of his penance. "So my soul has yet to arrive in a body where it might be saved. I await the time when it leaves this last tunic and returns to Heaven."

━━━

"The mending of soles is my profession," a cobbler announced. "The instinct to quit this earth is no match for worn leather, this much I do know. Your lady, *bon homme,* tried to fly before she had learnt how to walk. The feet, *bon homme,* are the only means we have to make the long journey to heaven."

━━━

"God and the Virgin Mary are none other than the world we see and hear," a Cathar peasant from Caussou remarked, knowing that his senses would not betray him.

These remarks were made by people who possessed only the ragtags of a consciously realized belief. Sincere in their expression, however, they announced to anyone with an ear for heresy that they wished to distance themselves from established Church doctrine. They had allowed their loyalty to a place, to the past, and to an earthy dogma nurtured among the rugged valleys of the Pyrenees to influence their thinking. Not for them the rarefied doctrine of the Church Fathers hammered out by way of disputation and argument.

I decided to visit the tower in which the inquisitor had once conducted his court. In this austere interior countless carefully prepared dossiers had been presented in evidence against those accused of heresy. The intransigent had been condemned to death at the stake; others who recanted had been jailed, fined, or sentenced to wearing the yellow cross. An odor of sanctity continued to permeate the room, mingling with a distinctly sulfurous smell.

Inside the building I came upon a room dominated by a central pillar. Chains used to secure the prisoners were still attached to its stonework. Beneath this room, down a winding staircase, I discovered a cell where the heretics were once tortured. In my mind I could hear the voices of the accused, bewildered in their belief, answering questions designed to force them to confess.

"Rooms like this one remind us of how much we have lost in the name of protecting what we believe," a voice beside me spoke.

I turned to see a woman, in her late thirties perhaps, elegantly dressed but in an informal sort of way, wearing a distracted and yet intelligent look on her face. She was basking in sunlight slanting through an arrow slit in a far wall.

"I suppose we have all found ourselves confronting the inquisitor at some time in our lives."

"As our conscience, perhaps," the woman responded, anticipating what I had not the temerity to say.

"You are, I gather, a student of local history. Such rooms conjure up unpleasant memories."

"The Cathars were our last hope, monsieur. They chose a form of belief that they had created for themselves. Of course, to many theologians, its doctrine was not particularly original. We know that it had traveled from afar on the lips of merchants and so became garbled en route. We know too this gnostic doctrine was discussed around village hearths, in the secrecy of family hovels, and was never subject to critical thought as it was with Church dogma. It was, after all, a furtive doctrine, a renegade jostling for the hearts and minds of men and women bent upon breaking with the power of the pope. Though it may not have been subtle, and encouraged certain extreme forms of behavior, at least it brought people together in the spirit of fraternity and love. Rome could never take this away from the Cathars, monsieur. It never did, and never will."

"You speak as if the doctrine still lives."

"Monsieur," the woman confessed. "I come from the small village of Montaillou in the foothills of the Pyrenees. My forebears were the last to submit to the Inquisition. They were rounded up in 1320 and condemned to the stake or imprisonment. With their deaths a certain spirit was extinguished, snuffed out like a candle. Yet their memory lives on in their descendants."

I didn't know quite how to reply.

"Let me tell you of a dream I had when I was a girl. I saw two men, both Cathars, reclining on the bank of a stream. One man fell asleep, while the other remained awake. Suddenly the watcher noticed a small lizard emerge from the mouth of his friend. The lizard scuttled down to the stream and crossed to the other side on a branch.

"On the far side, and visible to the observer, the skull of an ass was lodged in the earth. The lizard approached it, then ran in and out of the skull's eyes. Finally the lizard returned to the stream, only to find that the branch was gone, swept away by the current.

"Meanwhile the sleeper began to thrash about. He was unable to wake up, in spite of his friend's help. Realizing what was amiss, the watcher hurried down and placed another branch across the stream. This the lizard scuttled across and reentered the sleeping man's mouth. The man awoke and told his friend of a strange dream.

"'I dreamed that I was crossing a bridge,' the man explained. 'I entered a great palace with many towers and sumptuous rooms. When I wished to return, however, I found that the bridge had disappeared! If I attempted to swim the river I would be drowned. That was the reason why I thrashed about in my sleep. Until the bridge was rebuilt, I knew I couldn't return at all—or even wake up.'"

"Are you able to interpret the dream?" I asked.

"For years the dream remained a mystery," the woman continued. "During the course of my life I married and pursued a career, without ever really understanding what the dream meant. Not knowing its meaning affected all that I did or thought. Happiness, love, and success continued to elude me all those years."

"Have you found the peace you were looking for?"

"Actually, a gentleman in this very city gave me the answer," replied the woman, her face still aglow from the sun streaming through the arrow slit. "A keen student of heresy, and an Arabic scholar as well, he was able to interpret my dream."

"And?"

"Of course the lizard is my soul, monsieur. It remains in the body at all times. But it does, on occasions, like to wander free, quitting the body and wandering in and out of death. If it finds itself unable to return, owing to some deep trauma, then its absence engenders extreme distress. The dream was telling me that my soul had quit my body as a child, and until the scholar provided me with the key, I had been left to thrash about in a kind of daze, awake but still asleep.

"I went on this way for much of my life. Then I came to realize that buried in my dream was the entire doctrine of Catharism. I had been dreaming of my heritage and my family's past, without ever being aware of it. Heresy was in my very bones—no, outside my body—trying to return. The scholar advised me to honor this knowledge and allow it to reenter me as a friend."

"A remarkable story," I said. "I feel that I have journeyed all this way, and accepted every detour offered, as if I too were that lizard abandoned on the far riverbank."

I explained to the woman my reasons for being in Aquitaine, my obsession with Marcebru and his death roll, and my preoccupation with Amedée de Jois. The woman listened sympathetically, encouraging me to continue. Without realizing it at first, my confession had drawn us closer together. For a mo-

ment we had become confidants, or—dare I say it?—
white friends.

"Monsieur," the woman confided, her casual elegance now a kind of uniform. "Let me give you the address of the scholar I mentioned. Normally he does not welcome visitors, but I believe he will make an exception in your case. Your interests coincide. What you have already discovered will be of interest to him too."

The woman produced a visiting card from her purse and handed it to me. I read the inscription:

Prof. Jean-Paul de Langue
gens frairina

31 Rue Quartier
Saint-Nazaire
Carcassonne, Ocitan

"*Gens frairina?*" I inquired.

"It means 'the Brotherhood.' What it implies, however, I am unable to tell you," the woman advised.

"He gives his residence as Ocitan, not France."

"As far as I am aware, Professor de Langue lives in an imaginary country. When you meet him you will understand."

We shook hands. The woman smiled as we parted, the sun still an arrow of light on her back.

19

THE BROTHERHOOD

—

Iɴ ᴍʏ ᴘᴏssᴇssɪᴏɴ was a visiting card directing me to the house of Jean-Paul de Langue, an Arabic scholar and a member of some obscure brotherhood. An element of conspiracy, of covert thought, had become a part of my exploration now. I was no longer following a simple trail blazed across Aquitaine by Marcebru's death roll. Its contents, once so familiar an emissary of expression, had begun to reflect something entirely different. It had become a document pronouncing a particular kind of *danger.*

Dipping into its pages after dinner that evening, I found myself slowly enveloped by its artful deceit. Love was on the minds of Marcebru's correspondents, but indeed no ordinary love. A certain passion embellished their prose, making it shine more brilliantly than if it had been subject to the gloss of words.

"Pure love consists in the contemplation of the mind married to the affection of the heart. It binds the hearts of lovers with every feeling of delight. Fulfillment comes to those who reject the comeliness of Venus," wrote Arnaut, a jongleur returning to the court of Toulouse.

———

"There is only one kind of love that is pure," another poet urged. "It goes as far as the kiss and the embrace, and modest contact with the nude lover. Ah, the exquisite pleasure of abandoning the final solace! All excellence of character springs forth from such an adventure. Neither maid, widow, nor wife can be corrupted by such a love. They, like he, find themselves on the brink of an immaculate life when they plunge into this storm."

———

"It is no sin to commit this kind of adultery," Alanus de Insulis wrote. "Beyond all possession, it craves a union between minds disenfranchised of their desires. You, Marcebru, who have ventured into the enemy's terrain and brought back its standards—you know the meaning of *fin' amistatz plevida**

---

* Prov. "the purest of loves."

more than most. Spain, oh! glutton for punishment. Was it not you who announced:

Ah, pure love, font of good
Which illumines the world.

or:

As wine comes from grapes,
So is a man ennobled by love."

━━━━

"Love is like a swallow: it flies south during winter, and returns wearied by its journey. There it alights on her bed and studies her sleeping limbs. 'Practice pure love with me,' it twitters, 'now that the distance between us has been consumed.' That day the felicity of passion silenced all reproach," wrote a poacher from Ariège.

These men were talking about a love that clearly was more refined than one of sensuality. They were talking of a love motivated by a desire to intensify selfhood beyond the point of mere gratification, so that it might join lovers more closely. It was a curious sentiment, not at all in keeping with Catholicism or an earlier Classical view of love. Ovid's careful articulation of sensual love bore little relation to the idea of restraint that so permeated *fin' amors*.

Why was it so important for lovers to abstain from intimacy? What did they hope to gain by orchestrating their desires and then suppressing them? Did such emotions spring from Catharism and its disdain for the flesh, or from Catholicism and its abhorrence of the carnal? Or was it simply that unfulfilled desire gave to life a piquancy that neither war nor religious ecstasy could replace?

Knowing that whatever had inspired Marcebru to dedicate the death roll to the memory of Amedée de Jois depended on answering these questions, I decided to visit M. de Langue in the morning.

His apartment was located on the second floor of a building whose implacable stonework reminded me of a fortress. Gazing up at its windows, I half expected to be accosted with boiling oil and arrows. I climbed the staircase to the landing in front of M. de Langue's door. It had been tiled in the fashion of a Moorish courtyard.

I knocked. There was no response. Accepting this silence as a rebuttal, I started down the stairs. Then a voice addressed me from above:

"Monsieur. Forgive my tardiness. I was, so to speak, absent. Please, you are welcome."

I looked up. A man stood by the balustrade. He was slightly built, wispy in appearance, wearing what appeared to be a caftan. A white goatee accentuated the angularity of his face. Deep-set eyes suggested a remoteness in his manner, as if the man spent a good deal of his time wandering far from his body.

I was ushered into his apartment, a place of austerity and muted light. The living room looked like a Bedouin tent. Carpets were strewn on the floor, inlaid brass tables on ornate wooden stands vied with bookstands to catch the eye, and embroidered pillows lay against the walls. The only concession to the life of a scholar was a wall of books, many of which were written in Arabic. I had entered the domain of a dervish.

We discussed generalities for a while. M. de Langue expressed interest in my journey. He knew of the man's work through his own studies. I gathered from his remarks that his special field of interest was the influence of Hispano-Arabic literature on medieval thought. He saw links between the troubadour lyric, the Moorish poets, and the ideas of Islamic philosophers such as Averroes and Avicenna, which had penetrated European thought.

"The Pyrenees acted as a placenta to Europe," he confided. "France, and indeed all Europe, were nourished by the ideas of Islam brought over the narrow mountain trails by visitors from Moorish Spain. Even today we all bathe in the reflected light of the crescent moon."

"Such an idea might be considered anathema to many," I ventured.

"In our current climate of orthodoxy, perhaps. But in the twelfth century kings, nobles, and sages all yearned to conquer Palestine in the name of Christ. It was a philosophic yearning as much as it was a desire to reclaim Jerusalem for the Faith. This confrontation between cross and crescent inevitably resulted in a contest of rich import. In spite of the pious name-calling of the age, men of learning on both sides of the Pyrenees came to respect the beliefs of their enemies. The Arabs absorbed the ideas of the ancient Greeks, and European scholars drank at the fountain of Arab mysticism."

"A quid pro quo of thought," I suggested.

"Which brings us to Marcebru and Amedée de Jois," M. de Langue replied, drawing near to him a bookstand with a text lying open between its arms. "Their love goes to the heart of the conflict between body and mind that has plagued philosophers. Such is the uncompromising nature of *fin' amors*. It imposes the death sentence on all who practice it."

"Like certain insects which kill their partner after copulation, true lovers when they love must die."

M. de Langue placed a hand on the open text at his elbow.

"Let me tell you a story," he began, "about a Bedouin tribe known as the Bani Odhrah. Tradition tells of their young women being beautiful and their men of unexampled purity. It was said of these people that when they loved they died."

"Such a thing isn't possible, surely."

"Shall I read from this book, or is your mind already closed to its possibility?" M. de Langue gently reprimanded.

"I'm sorry. Please continue," I said.

"It was told how Djamil, an Odhrahi youth, fell in love with a young Bedouin girl named Buthania. One dark night, after repeated attempts to meet her alone, he finally managed to do so. They talked for hours as lovers sometimes do, until Djamil, unable to suppress his feelings for Buthania any longer, begged her to submit to his caresses. The young woman refused his plea, reminding him of the transitory nature of passion and the threat of divine punishment. Shamed and confused, Djamil was forced to apologize.

"In spite of Djamil's rejection by Buthania's father, they continued to see one another in secret. The father, in turn, married off his daughter to a certain Nubaith, hoping that their love might die. But still Djamil and Buthania met at night, by the cold light of the moon, to share their love. Angered by their liaison, her kinsmen stirred up the authorities against Djamil, forcing him to flee. He took to a life of a wandering minstrel, singing love songs, until he eventually died in Egypt, some say of a broken heart. All we are left with of their love are recollections of those who attended their last meeting.

"According to these reports, Buthania slipped away with her companions to the concealment of the palm trees one night. There Djamil was waiting for her. Nor did they separate until dawn was upon them. Of that fateful meeting, Djamil later wrote: 'Buthania said to me that unless I leave at once, her brother and father would capture me. Struck by fear, I began to retire, only to see her smile. I knew then that she would never surrender me to her kinsmen. I took her by the ringlets of her hair and kissed her lips. The pleasure they gave me was like that of a throat parched with intoxication, sipping cool water from a spring.'

"Later, when he lay dying in Egypt, Djamil called for his friend, Ibn Sahl, that he might make his confession: 'What would you say of a man who never drank wine, who never committed fornication or murder, who never stole, and who honored God?' Ibn Sahl replied: 'Such a man will surely enter paradise.' Then his friend asked: 'Who is this man?' To which Djamil answered: 'That man is myself.' Ibn

Sahl responded, 'In the name of Allah, how can you say this when for the past twenty years you have celebrated the charms of Buthania?'

"Monsieur," M. de Langue raised his head briefly, and directed his remark to me. "Djamil's reply goes to the heart of the relationship between Marcebru and his *fin' amors*. 'Now that I am about to die,' Djamil said, 'may I be deprived of the intercession of Muhammad if I so much as placed a hand on her with improper intention."

"Are you suggesting Djamil feared divine retribution if he had made love to Buthania?" I asked.

"Not at all. His actions lay beyond the censure of any injunction proscribed by custom or law, or even God. Djamil was only interested in preserving their love. He knew that to possess her sexually amounted to an empty cup. He was content with a word, the mere sight of Buthania, the infrequency of their meetings, a rare kiss. Their love became an elixir more potent than life.

"In the end it was Buthania who gave Djamil his reason for dying," M. de Langue continued. "At their last meeting before he had escaped to Egypt, and while he was pleading with Buthania to restore his reason so that he might one day lead a normal life, she replied: 'Your death is deeply rooted in you now, and will grow. Whatever you desire is beyond your reach. Accept this.'"

"How could he, knowing that separation would bring perpetual pain?" I argued.

"The practice of courtly love involves the death of the beloved. This is its only release," M. de Langue responded.

"So Amedée de Jois didn't die by her own hand to escape her body, but so as to be released from the bonds of *fin' amors*."

"A valid, if unpalatable assumption."

"Why do you think so?"

"Are any of us prepared to die to preserve intact a love we have acquired by a supreme act of restraint?"

"Of course not. The only death we idealize today is one derived from excess," I reasoned.

M. de Langue's tale had opened a gate for me. Beyond lay a plain populated by values I had never considered before. I had journeyed to Aquitaine in pursuit of more conventional reasons for Marcebru's behavior in the wake of Amedée de Jois's death. Unrequited passion, rebuttal, an obsessive spiritual malaise, even a tragic love—these were the issues I had wanted to explore. They were, if not obvious, at least explainable.

M. de Langue's interpretation changed the entire nature of the argument. His story of Djamil and

Buthania intimated a way of thinking that went beyond desire, passion, sexual fulfillment, even jealousy. The Bedouin lovers hinted at a love that always remained within the realm of the concrete. So completely were they bound to one another, however, that the only way they could escape the shackles of nonpossession was in death. It was this death that Marcebru had chosen to make the basis of his own grief, since it opened the way for him to explore the quenching of desire as the beginning of true detachment.

M. de Langue interrupted my thoughts. "The fact is, monsieur, by their actions they have given us something unique."

"In what way?" I asked. "No, don't answer. I think I already know."

"To please a solitary such as myself, I trust you will grant me the benefit of your conclusions."

"M. de Langue," I began, sensing that what I had to say might augment our friendship, "you have placed your whole life at the service of scholarship. As you are aware, we often make assumptions too quickly about the origin of our ideas, our beliefs, and our culture. I had always believed that Marcebru had taken to the road to assuage his grief at the loss of his *fin' amors*, and that language was his staff. But now I'm not so certain."

"Words may act as a camouflage. They sometimes disguise meaning, concealing what they are meant to reveal."

"Yet how otherwise can one describe what you have related to me without words?"

"It is a mystery that I am unable to fathom," replied M. de Langue, closing the book. "To do so may well lead to their extinction."

"So you are advising me to draw back from the brink."

"Language *is* brinkmanship, monsieur. It is the art of circling a light in darkness. Light and language are like twins, identical and yet different. Our task is to find a way that allows them to reflect in one another's glory."

"M. de Langue, your visiting card suggests that you belong to an institution called *gens frairina.* Is this a sect, a brotherhood, or merely a fraternity of like minds?"

"It is, monsieur, a singular association," responded the man, lost in the folds of his caftan. "You see, only I and my thoughts are its members."

"It is an order for yourself alone?"

"Where else can one go to share the most solitary of professions?"

"Scholarship always has its friends. There are networks, conferences, university colleges, and learned journals to which one is able to contribute."

"Like Marcebru, I must remain a solitary member of an organization whose task is to remonstrate with defeat."

"Love, a defeat? I find this hard to accept."

"*Victoire,* my friend, lies in overcoming even this," replied M. de Langue, savoring the intimacy of the word in French.

I realized then that the man had inducted me in his *gens frairina,* another searcher in pursuit of the artifice of words.

———

20

A LETTER
FROM A FRIEND

—

WHAT WAS THE POINT of going on? I asked myself. It was as if M. de Langue had wanted to forestall any further inquiry, given his reservations with regard to the power of words. Yet I knew that language was the one instrument available to myself and Marcebru. In the end I began to believe that M. de Langue was challenging us to a dialogue without words. Was this the only way left for us—to turn our backs on communication and become a society of one?

His Bedouin tent had become a *tekke,* a secret meeting place in the desert. He and Djamil were of like mind, abandoning bliss as being little more than a station along the way. More significantly, he, Djamil, and Amedée de Jois had chosen a similar path—a path whose destination was a form of death-in-life, since all of them had removed themselves from the heart's affections in various ways.

I had never expected to be offered this as an alternative. Indeed, I preferred to tread the path of language as a key to life rather than relinquish contact with the word. It was, after all, the only tool I possessed that might help to free me from the bondage of not-knowing.

Yet M. de Langue's advice had clearly helped the young woman I had met in the inquisitor's tower. She now knew who she was. Heresy, the eternal diatribe against absolutism that had split a nation, was in her bones. She knew that to disagree with orthodoxy was fundamental to her origins. That this right was lost to her by forgetting the past was of no consequence anymore. M. de Langue had pointed her in the direction of silently assuming her legacy as a Cathar as a way of rediscovering herself.

Now, it seemed, there were three members of the Brotherhood, not one. Or perhaps four, if one included Marcebru. It was a dream, this society of solitaries, a place where language could be dismantled to extract its power of deliverance. Knowing that Buthania had offered Djamil his reason for dying made me realize that I was dealing with an age-old problem: Does the nature of our death grow in us in relation to the life we lead, or is it rooted in us from the beginning?

Meanwhile, a letter from my old friend Horace

Winterton was waiting for me when I returned to my hotel. I tore it open. Of all the people I knew, he was the only one capable of helping me solve this problem.

My Dear Friend,

Of late, I have been spending my time by the river at Kew consulting with the seven wise men on your behalf. Their feathers, as you can imagine, remain forever unruffled. I do not know why some creatures are blessed with the appearance of being so assuredly right for this world, while others find it so hard to justify their worth. It is no accident that swans tend to regard us quizzically, since they have never grown used to our desire to revere them. As Nietzsche says, while we blink their nobility escapes us.

Avicenna, one of the greatest Arabic philosophers, believed that the role of learning depended upon the ascent of one's soul to the Agent Intelligence, the ruler of the tenth and last celestial sphere in the order of intelligences emanating from above. I happen to agree with him; but then, as you know, I have always been seduced by such elegant systems of thought. Yet even he found it impossible to explain what he meant except through allegory. In the end he abandoned metaphysics for metaphor.*

---

* Avicenna's concept of the Agent Intelligence found echoes in Saint Thomas Aquinas's *De anima,* where he suggests that

He told a story of how he accompanied a band of hunters who went forth to snare birds. Quite a number of these birds succumbed to the hunters' bait and were trapped in their nets, including himself. Like them, he soon found himself confined to a cage where time dragged and memory of his former freedom pricked his conscience. After a while even he grew accustomed to imprisonment.

Some of the birds managed to escape, however, thus alerting him to his predicament. He asked them to teach him how to escape too, which they did. With their help he was able to join them in their flight homeward. On their way back they encountered eight high mountains, six of which they managed to fly over after persistent effort. On the seventh, they reached the summit and rested. Before them was a view of unexampled beauty and plenty.

By the time they had attained the summit of the eighth mountain, its peak lay in cloud. There too they

---

union gives the soul contact with absolute beauty, absolute goodness, and true elegance. The aptitude of the soul for such union is actualized by learning, knowledge, and science. It is achieved by an emanation from the Agent Intelligence, an illumination by which the Agent Intelligence, which contains the models and principles of the intelligible world, confers the forms on the soul. "Just as the sun is actually visible in itself and makes actually visible what was visible only *in potentia,* so the Agent Intelligence is actually intelligible in itself and makes intelligible what was before intelligible only *in potentia.*"

encountered immaculately colored birds who guided them through the mist to the palace of the Great King. During their audience with him they described their miserable condition and pleaded for his help. He at once ordered a messenger to approach them and strike off the chains still attached to their legs. The philosopher realized that the messenger was none other than the angel of death.

Avicenna described the Great King in detail. He represented the union of all that can be imagined. Beauty and an all-consuming perfection dominated his demeanor. It became clear to the philosopher that the Great King was none other than the Agent Intelligence, that sphere of excellence which can be reached only after much struggle.

Of course this story has a moral. I will not trouble to elucidate it for you, knowing your penchant for exploring these matters in your own way. Suffice to say, my dear friend, this story goes to the heart of Catharism and its desire to shrug off all that inhibits. Which leads me to speculate that Amedée de Jois had discovered what she must do in order to earn the Great King's praise.

Why I relate Avicenna's tale is that I believe your own researches will have already led you to a similar conclusion: Marcebru and his fin' amors had embarked upon a course of action that precluded them ever being together, except in memory. Death offered them an intensity of experience not otherwise achievable. Life with its fetters had to be struck off if affinity with the Agent Intelligence was to be enjoyed.

You and I, my dear friend, are captives of speculative knowledge. We cannot shrug off its chains. So we wander the back roads of the past, keep company with dead poets, pry into their lives. We are voyeurs, content to identify with the risk that others take on our behalf. It is the affliction of our age. None of us, I'm afraid, have the courage to fly over those mountains, or to request an audience with the Great King. The angel of death is no friend of ours.

I make these remarks in the light of the impasse that you may have reached in your endeavor. Shall I tell you that the swans came to your rescue? Gazing at their whiteness, at their supreme indifference to the emptiness that surrounds them on this bright afternoon, I sensed their unease nonetheless. They were telling me that flight is all but impossible, save for one whose wings are well waxed in the interest of taunting the sun. Then, they seem to imply, and only then, could one expect to encounter the glory of the abyss.

I remain your cordial friend, slightly ruffled of course, but still feathered,

Horace Winterton

I finished the letter. It dawned upon me that, like M. de Langue, who had retreated to the silence of his Bedouin tent in his own apartment, Horace had taken another name not so much to escape the guilt of the past but because of his desire to reaffirm the power of renewal that anonymity conferred.

Solitude is a difficult encampment. Its guy ropes grow rigid on frosty mornings. People retreat to it when they have need of succor. Men like my friend Horace and M. de Langue had found a way of defining the limits of their world by engrossing themselves in what Avicenna called the Agent Intelligence. As the Great King, this realm had made them its messengers. The summit of knowledge lay before them, an ornament of faith in the power of the mind. For them, real death lay in the renunciation of all that made desire possible.

"The soul is a solitary substance," I recalled Aquinas's words. "Joined to the body by a natural affection, it is located between two worlds—the world of mind and that of matter. It is drawn upward by speculation and downward by action." Thus it wanders through space, a lonely at times disfigured star, torn this way and that as it struggles to maintain its course. It occurred to me that the Brotherhood was a society not of one, two, three, or perhaps even four members, but of the very singularity of being itself.

I had come to see my journey in Marcebru's footsteps as something of a dream. I was wrong. Nor was it simply a matter of language giving ground to any nuance that happened to be provoked by my own subjectivity or feelings. It had gone beyond that now—beyond love, death, grief, and the survival of the poem. What I had begun to encounter was a bitter harvest of words unleashed upon the green lands of Aquitaine by those who, in the past, had failed to understand their importance.

Meanwhile, I had come to Aquitaine acting as a historian, as an archaeologist, and had found myself adopting the role of a metaphysician, asking questions that had no definite answers. I felt empty, a philosopher manqué who longed to hear the truth stated just once, simply and with elegance.

I almost wished I could escape my predicament. This roll of parchment, abandoned in a frozen river long ago, had disrupted my thoughts, my very well-being. I was left to wander about from place to place, a vagabond all but blind to the obvious: that buried in these words, in the opinions and beliefs collected by Marcebru on his journey, was something I couldn't yet see. They too were a form of camouflage.

21

RIVER OF GOLD

—

MINING was uppermost in my mind as I drove on to Foix, once a place of strong Cathar sympathies under the rule of Count Raymond-Roger. It was here that his sister Esclarmonde had presided as a Perfect over this isolated mountain town. The surrounding region was once noted for the richness of its iron ore, extracted by miners working in association with muleteers. In days past these men would purchase the miners' hods and carry them down the valley to the foundries.

Simon de Montfort was careful never to attack Foix during his campaign against the heretics. The Treaty of Paris in 1229, however, forced Count Raymond to acknowledge his fealty to the king of France, thus signaling the beginning of the end to the Albigensian Crusade. In its heyday, however, the court of Foix was a haven for heretics and troubadours. Esclarmonde and her sister-in-law offered protection to all those trying to escape the inquisitor. Nor were they afraid to debate with visiting clerics the merits of their doctrine.

On the way I stopped for a glass of wine and a sandwich in the town of Fanjeaux. Built on a spur of rock from which there was a fine view over the Lauragais Plain and Montaigne Noire, the town was a sacred spot in Roman times. Its name is derived from *fanum jovis,* meaning "Temple of Jupiter."

Saint Dominic visited Fanjeaux in his early days of preaching against heresy. He settled in the hamlet of Prouille in April 1207, where he established a small religious community of women converts. Later a group of monks took up residence in the hilltop town. According to legend, Dominic chose Prouille to live in after witnessing three visions of a fireball descending upon the hamlet from a nearby promontory.

Fire was a theme that ran through many of the legends associated with Dominic's attempts to convert the Cathars. In the local chapel dedicated to him, a roof beam is preserved as a reminder of a miracle associated with his ministry. On a winter's day spent debating with the Cathars, Dominic handed one of his adversaries a document summarizing his arguments in defense of orthodoxy. The Cathar returned to his host's house that afternoon and threw the document into the fire. It refused to burn. Three times he threw it into the hearth, but on each occasion it flew up from the flames and hung suspended on the ceiling, scorching the beam that is now housed in the chapel.

The extraordinary beauty of these mountain valleys seemed to bear no relationship to the deep and prolonged discord that had afflicted this region. The miners and weavers, the shepherds and muleteers, the tailors and cobblers, the host of men and women who had inhabited these valleys in Marcebru's day— they all had struggled to survive here in the face of war and famine.

Marcebru had passed this way on his trek north. He had stayed in Cathar villages and listened to the villagers talk around communal hearths. He had asked those who could to write down their comments in his death roll as they churned butter or repaired worn jerkins by candlelight. For these folk would have heard tell of the belt found under Amedée's habit when she died; such news travels fast when it concerned one of their own.

"I have never believed in the resurrection of the body after death," wrote Guillaume, a farmer near Pamiers. "Though they preached it in church, I did not believe it! When we die, I know our body is dissolved into earth and ashes. But I believe in the survival of the soul. The wicked shall be thrown over rocks and precipices by demons."

━━━━

"Have a care when you are walking," Gelis, a quarry man from Ax, wrote, "not to throw your arms and legs about. Keep your elbows by your side, otherwise you may knock over a ghost. Remember, we walk unwittingly among a multitude of spirits. Invisible are they but to the messengers of souls."

━━━━

"I have heard it said that they carve with axes statues of saints in the house of idols [i.e., a church]," wrote Bernard Gombert of Ax-les-Thermes. "For them, the Virgin is never anything but a piece of wood, without real eyes, feet, ears, or mouth."

━━━━

"It is true, our Perfects have as much power to absolve sins as had the Apostles Peter and Paul. Those who follow them go to heaven, the rest to hell," wrote Raymond Vayssière, a stock breeder from the region of Arques.

━━━━

"Amedée de Jois carried a secret. Though she died in Saint-Martin, we believe she was one of us. She knew that God is none other than God's silence remaining silent," a Perfect named Gauzia wrote.

———

"We are doomed as soon as we begin to regard life as our sole obsession," the chatelaine of Tarascon announced.

———

"She possessed a broken identity derived from an initial laceration, source of the multiple, good and evil," a village matriarch called Belote added.

The road was often steep and winding, and I slowed down to negotiate the bends. Beyond, the Pyrenees rose in undulating hills to the high mountains, their summits already whitened by early snow. This old glacial valley of jagged bluffs and ruined towers reminded me of an abandoned chess table in a village square.

As I came around a turn, a man walking along the roadside caused me to brake suddenly. Slung over his shoulder he carried what appeared to be a large bowl, a pan perhaps. Initially I thought it a hat. He wore dirty trousers and a rough check shirt, its sleeves rolled up to the elbows. His boots were laced with leather thongs. Hanging about his waist was a bedroll.

As I drew level with him, the man gave a friendly

wave. I decided to stop and offer him a lift. Before I could say anything he had tossed his gear, including the large pan, on the back seat and climbed in beside me.

"Merci, m'sieur," he said in a thick, provincial French accent.

"I couldn't help noticing that pan," I inquired, my curiosity getting the better of me.

"Moi, je suis un orpailleur," confided the man.

"A gold panner?" I said, surprised. "Is there still gold in these parts?"

"I come from a long tradition, m'sieur. The sandy river bed of the Ariège has sparkled since the time of the troubles," the man added, alluding to the Albigensian Crusade. "Some call us *transparents,* the clear-seeing ones. We wander this sad and beautiful land, searching for what glitter remains in its gravel. We pan for those nuggets that bind memory to the earth. I am the last, m'sieur. The very last."

I was stuck by the curious mixture of poetry and fable in the man's speech. He spoke in a language at once ancient and mysterious. I didn't quite know how to respond. But I need not have worried: the man was content to continue his conversation as if I had already plied him with questions.

"There is no steelier point than the point of infinity, m'sieur. Look at me, eh? Untempted by most things save gold dust and what lies beyond extremes.

You think words are illusory because they are attached to your desire to arrest time? I tell you, there's no steelier point than our point of view. Boredom, yes boredom is our greatest fear; variety our greatest vice."

His staccato of statements, hard and bright, ricocheted around the car.

"There are too many of us," the gold panner announced as we threaded our way among autumn leaves by the road. "Yes, there's too many living on this earth. The more of us there are, the more images of the divine we find in nature. Confusion reigns."

"Monsieur le orpailleur," I began, trying to instill some order into our conversation. "You are a gold panner. I gather from what you say that you have been one all your life. Presumably your father taught you your trade, and the streams of this region constitute your workplace. In all weather you have waded in pools, pan in hand, trying to extract a few specks from an exhausted river system. I may say, without wishing to offend you, that as the last of your kind, you are probably an anachronism."

"I am from the museum of life," the man agreed. "For me, every nugget that I discover is a sort of poem. I pan for them with the same yearning as the poet for his *fin' amors*. By rock pools I patiently await their gestation. Gold, you see, is not just dense matter; it is the poem of place. How it glitters celebrates this country that I love. I pan for the beauty of my homeland."

I was reminded of Marcebru's attempt to write the perfect poem, one that would change the world.

"All of us seek it, m'sieur," the gold panner continued, as if reading my thoughts. "People have died for it too. No, died *from* it. The perfect poem is a divine disease. It spreads through our limbs, fills up our veins to bursting point, enters our thoughts like a cavalcade."

"You believe it's possible to write one?"

"Words, my friend, are flecks of gold among gravel. They glitter amid all that is inert. The poet carefully works his pan, washing away the impurities, thereby allowing the specks to remain. He gathers these together, the heaviest of residues, and fuses them. It is this fusion that gives us what we most desire."

"You mean, perfection?" I said, thinking of Esclarmonde and all the other Perfects who had tried to cleanse themselves of their frailties.

"As I said, m'sieur, words are pure gold. They are shadow's work, the ore of our consuming lack."

The gold panner went on, speaking in riddles. His comments seemed the product of a mind half deranged. But as his muddled remarks settled in my mind, I started to see how he and Marcebru were kinsmen of sorts. His one desire was to recapture those countless mournful images that make up the memory of what we lack. I became confused myself by his remarks, if only because he appeared to see no difference between his own profession and that of the poet.

"Poetry, m'sieur, can only be found in that pool of the unforeseen. It is the clear splash of invisibility upon stone," the gold panner remarked as we approached Foix. A castle stood on a hill overlooking the town, its keep as cylindrical as a rook. Then he suddenly changed the subject. "You travel to Montségur, the Cathar stronghold, no? What awaits you there is the last page in a book. It is the book of shared deaths."

"I gather you mean the place where a people were martyred for their beliefs," I replied, beginning to understand the man's train of thought for the first time.

"Belief is not the last act of martyrdom, m'sieur. Denouncing it is."

———

22

IN THE STREETS
OF FOIX

—

W<small>E</small> ENTERED THE OUTSKIRTS of the city rather slowly. Its red-slated roofs reflected the last rays of the sun, resisting their warmth. The narrow windows in the houses reminded me of the town's long history of introspection as they continued to repel the curious eye. The place had suffered a great deal during the Inquisition and was not about to give up its secrets easily.

It was here in Foix, however, that the death roll had finally descended from the rocky stronghold of the Pyrenees and begun its long journey in search of answers.

As I left him by the roadside, the gold panner kindly directed me to a pension. He waved to me as I departed. In my rearview mirror I saw him as he shouldered his pan, which shone like an orb in the late afternoon sunlight. Gold was in his grasp, if only as a measure of autumnal light.

I had no desire to leave my room that evening,

not even for the purpose of visiting a restaurant. Only the death roll had the power to satisfy my desire for nourishment. I carried it about with me as I might a menu souvenired from some hotel.

Instead of food that evening, I wanted more. I wanted to be consumed by fervor, that deep gesture of the heart toward overcoming itself. I took up the death roll and once more read in its text the memories of those who had known the meaning of hunger:

"Dear heart, sanction this escape from any distinction between act and acceptance," wrote a Perfect from Foix. "What I long for is release from the hiddenness of my own will."

———

"Our nature receives its imprint from its own instinct toward consorting with what is noble," a guildsman of the city remarked. "She, the jewel of Canigou, allowed her own release to wax and wane as does a candle before an icon of Our Lady. Nothing existed for her save the beauty of her own demise."

———

"Poet, taste fear. Almonds are no match for its exquisite tartness. I who bear in my cart all manner of cloth from Byzantium, I offer you the shroud of your own annulment. Its thread is none other than that of identity clinging to the illusion of its own immortality. Deep is the resonance of him who chooses his own way," wrote a merchant from Padua, traveling to the court of Castile to sell his wares.

———

"In life possibility is as deceitful as any siren," a wandering mason remarked.

———

"I knew of a pelican whose feathers shone like the sun," Na Ferriara, a healer from Prades d'Allion wrote. "Leaving its young in the nest, it did so in order to follow the sun's path more freely. One day a fox climbed into its nest and tore out the chicks' claws. When this happened the pelican decided to hide its radiance and lie in wait for the fox among its own chicks. And so the pelican saved its young. In the same way Amedée de Jois hid her radiance under her own creation, better to protect it from the lowly instincts of survival."

———

"The interval between your footsteps set you apart," wrote a converted Jewess who dabbled in predictions. "Black cats did not stand by your body, so you are free of their taint. The shadow you cast is one of light against darkness."

Thus did the death roll announce its intention from the onset. It wanted to invest the memory of Amedée de Jois as representing something more than a mere record of condolences. Its task was to circumvent the bog of piety that normally presented itself in such documents, and to press forward along a different path.

I now realized that the death roll was intent upon its own journey; in the discovery of the highest silence whose meaning could never be expressed. Its destiny was to impose a sense of belonging upon Marcebru and all those who shared with him their feelings, including myself. We were joined by the prolixity of words and their hunger to express absolutes.

Like Marcebru, this document had been my companion for some weeks now. As close as we were to our destination, I felt we were beginning to grow more distant, if only because we were approaching the journey's beginning and so the prospect of separating for good. Between parchment and poet a chasm had begun to open up into which I had stumbled. Head over heels I was plummeting, grasping at expression. I knew that nothing could save me except an act of courage. I would have to climb that mountain from which Amedée de Jois had fallen, and discover for myself why she had chosen to do so.

——

23

MONTSÉGUR

H IGH ON A ROCKY PEAK the ruins of Montségur beckoned. The Cathar stronghold looked forlorn, its whitened battlements mottled as if by tear stains. It was here in 1244 that the last organized resistance by the Cathars was overcome by Raymond of Toulouse on the orders of Blanche of Castile. The Roman Catholic armies numbering ten thousand men laid siege to the fort between July 1243 and March 1244.

The attack had been provoked by the Cathars. One day a desperate band of heretics joined forces with others from Avignonette to ambush a party of inquisitors on their way to the town, where they planned to set up court. The inquisitors were all massacred. Raymond of Toulouse was blamed for organizing the plot. He tried to distance himself from the event by writing humble letters of submission to Blanche of Castile vowing vengeance on the murderers. Throughout 1243 and 1244 the fires of the Inquisition burned. Many of the nobility perished in the flames, including Pierre Robert of Mirepoix and the Dowager Lady of Fanjeaux.

The heretics fled to Lombardy, to Bosnia, or across the Pyrenees into Spain. Their remaining leaders gathered at Montségur, the mountain citadel where no Catholic had set foot for generations. The holy books of the Cathars were brought here for protection. For the most part farming folk who had succumbed to a belief that the rest of the world sought fit to denounce, the Cathars chose to defend their position to the death rather than become converts.

Under cover of darkness, patrols of experienced mountaineers scaled the steep cliff and, bypassing the fortress to the east, gained a foothold on the upper plateau. A ballista was hauled up the mountain in pieces, then assembled outside the walls of the citadel. Huge rocks were dug up from a nearby quarry to be used as projectiles. After a prolonged bombardment the walls were finally breached. Pierre Robert of Mirepoix, the Cathar leader, surrendered on condition that his tiny garrison was spared.

The Cathars were outnumbered. Men and

women alike took part in the defense. Even their most venerated bishops, men like the lord of Perelle and Guillebert of Castres, took up arms. When the end was near the greater part of the defenders received the *consolamentum,* the final rite of the Cathar church, which elevated them all to the rank of Perfects. By performing this ceremony they knew they had condemned themselves to death. The inquisitors' fires awaited them.

Though a truce had been declared, the Cathars were not a party to it. Rather than escape their fate, they seemed to welcome it. On the morning of 16 March 1244, 207 of them marched down from the citadel to the plain below and voluntarily climbed onto the huge pyre that had been prepared for them. This final act of *endura* spelled the end of the Cathars in Aquitaine. The fires that day consumed much more than a small band of Perfects; it reduced the idea of their resistance to ashes. From then on the Cathars survived as little more than an underground sect, landless, their holy books dispersed, their Perfects hounded into exile.

For the next ninety years the inquisitors continued their persecutions across Aquitaine until the movement was effectively crushed. The last burning of heretics, including one Perfect, took place in 1330. The defeat of the southern lords by the northern barons completed the process. All that survived this crusade was the melancholy gaiety of the troubadours.

On the Plain of the Martyrs I stopped to catch my breath before making the final ascent to the ruined citadel. A stele, erected in 1960 to celebrate the death of "those martyred in the name of pure Christian love," stood before me. I continued up the pathway toward the fortress, oblivious to the views of the Plantaurel ranges and the Aude Valley below. Amedée de Jois was on my mind, her death a silent echo among the dense pine trees at the foot of the crag.

Above, the ruins appeared more distant than ever against a cool blue sky. Perched on its peak, there was something vaguely theatrical about its setting. Chilled, and fatigued by my exertions, the thought arose in my mind that Montségur embodied the resplendency of the grave.

Marcebru was by my side as we made the final ascent. His words littered the pathway. I kept seeing the faceless image of him and Amedée de Jois I'd encountered back in Albi carved into the stonework. My journey with Marcebru had caused me to question every value that I possessed. I had been stripped of the self-confidence derived from knowledge. It all seemed so meaningless in the wake of funeral pyres and inquisitors. In the end it seemed that they, like myself, were the heretics, not the Cathars.

The track to the summit was steep. Lack of breath caused me to experience a mild attack of vertigo. Ascent and the solicitude of the condemned confronted me as I grabbed at tufts of grass. Montségur lay before me, its walls as gray as waste.

I entered the gate on the south side. Inside the courtyard were a number of dwellings where, according to my guidebook, the defenders had once sheltered. Access to the ramparts was through a narrow passage, which I climbed with difficulty. I passed beyond a room in which two arrow slits allowed the sun to shine through two more slits in the opposite wall on the day of the summer solstice. When I stood on the ramparts I noticed that the ribbon walls traced a five-pointed star, or pentagram, a symbol of both good and evil for the Cathars, since the upper single point reflected light, and the two points below Satan or darkness. The ancient symbolism continued to cling to these stones like mortar.

I gazed down at the distant valleys. I was standing on the roof of the world, a solitary climber, observing a view little changed from that chill March day in 1244 when the besieged Cathars prepared themselves to die. The great funeral pyre on the plain below, now a fierce cord of flame, intimated a silent gathering of Perfects ready to abandon the eternal round of lives to which they had been condemned.

I took out the death roll and read.

"Fire is the sun's laughter, the glow of future darkness. Harness its energy, as did Amedée de Jois when she quit the world," wrote Esperte, a Perfect from Tignac.

———

"Could the Word of God be silent in the face of such affliction? He has written an incomplete book, one that designates our death because we choose to believe in His power not to listen. *He* is the victim, since He has cast us adrift for daring to question Him. The stake is our haven, postillion of nurture, life's tree to which we cling so as to escape death," a deacon from Foix wrote.

———

"I do not fear the stake, Marcebru, not I! They can drive it through my heart for all I care, but I will not renounce my faith. Belief is a fertile field mowed by the angel of death. The scythe is life's best weapon since it alone can cut down whatever stands in its way," wrote Guillaume Fort from the village of Varilhes.

Beatrice de Planissoles wrote a short poem:

"He who said that being is beauty
Knew the task she had set herself
Submerged as she was in a grace
Eschewed by the hand of hope."

"For you, Marcebru, the perfect poem is but the furtive glow of embers that have already gone out. The inquisitor's fire holds no fear for us, for we too are committed to the final word," wrote the troubadour Arnaud Vital, defending a Cathar household in Ornolac.

"Obliteration is my heart's desire. Only then will I be released from the eternal round of lives, which has so bedeviled my soul," wrote Alazais, three days before she died by an act of *endura* in the village of Montgaillard.

"The theme of the perfect poem is annihilation," an anonymous voice wrote.

The poem, the funeral pyre, a ruin—they were all one. It was difficult to separate the word from the flame and its consummation. On this lonely mountain ghosts were abroad, clambering along passageways, peering through arrow slits at a world gone awry. They were the besieged. Failure had been their tombstone on which was inscribed a kind of victory.

Only now did I begin truly to understand what had motivated these people to sacrifice their lives. They, like Marcebru, were in league with loss, with the bright blade of severance. In this last gesture of defiance they had expressed all that they were and wanted to be. Nothing could replace the feeling of release that must have overcome them as the flames licked at their ankles. For once in their life they were aflame, a living torch of belief. It did not matter whether they were heretics because in the end they were free. All that mattered was the fire as they offered themselves up as tinder to its yearning.

———

24

AT CANIGOU

—

T HE A B B E Y Saint-Martin-du-Canigou stood on a rocky pinnacle above the village of Vernet-les-Bains, some distance away from Montségur, and at the cross-roads between Spain and France. Founded in the eleventh century, the monastery consisted of a number of residential blocks, a cloister, and a gallery overlooking a ravine. A lower church, dedicated to Our Lady of the Earth, formed the crypt of the upper church, with its barrel vaults and rugged, simply carved capitals dedicated to Saint Martin. A crenellated tower nestled by the church, its bells silenced by the imposing summit of Mount Canigou across the valley.

It took me nearly an hour to climb the narrow road to the Abbey, a popular pilgrimage spot for Catalan peasants in the past. There was a rustic air about the monastery in keeping with its simple piety. The abbey was no monument to theology or home to gilded manuscripts. Calm presided over the cloister, a sense of tranquillity; I could easily imagine Amedée de Jois living here, protected by these mountains, meditating in the frozen air of winter and cut off from the world by snowdrifts.

No one was there to meet me when I entered the cloister. Overlooking the ravine, I was able to survey the precipitous valleys that surrounded the abbey, knowing that I was gazing upon a clarity already partly obscured by the shadows cast by the Pyrenees. I had come upon a stream fed by melting snows.

A nun approached across the courtyard. She was dressed in a black habit, and white wings dominated her veil. In her mid-fifties, she wore rimless glasses and a large cross on her breast. The woman welcomed me with a smile, her hands outspread as if she were about to grasp mine. At the last moment she checked her gesture.

"Monsieur," she began, "Canigou welcomes all pilgrims. Do you plan to stay?"

"It was not my intention," I replied, surprised by her offer of hospitality.

"It's not often that we have visitors from afar. In autumn the tourists have already gone home to be by their fires. I am the guest mistress. My task is to make you feel comfortable."

The nun led me to a room in a building by the

cloister. From my window I looked out at the solitary peak of Mont Canigou. The room was furnished with a bed, a desk, one chair, and an icon of Our Lady on the wall. The worn stonework on the floor radiated prostrations and prayer. All the room's previous residents seemed to be there observing me as I tossed my backpack on the bed.

"At night it gets cold. I will bring extra blankets," the guest mistress said. "I presume you have come to speak with Sister Stephanie, our blessed abbess."

"If she can spare me the time," I replied, grateful for any excuse to stay.

"Abbess Stephanie will see you after supper in her rooms. I will escort you there."

With a slight bow the woman backed out of the room and was gone. I was left alone with my thoughts, the death roll, and a book of Marcebru's poems. I opened the latter at random and read:

> Saracen galleys may blockade
> Tripoli, citadel of our hope
> And guardian of *fin' amors*.
> Though in these days I see
> Meanness in flower, a paltry
> Bloom disguised as courtliness,
> And turn and twist like an eel
> In a net, never think that I,

Marcebru, will not sing
Of green meadows and fruit
Heavy on the branch.

All joy of the world is ours,
Lady, we bees in pursuit
Of pollen, the sweetness
Of love that brings us joy
And sadness when we part.
I sleep by your side, but
In distance do I preside
A prince of Outremer
Ready to be your knight
And your inspiration.
You grant me your life, and I
Place my heart at your service.

I closed the book, suddenly aware that Amedée de Jois was in the room, listening to the words of her *fin' amors* entreating her with his love. I imagined her walking the corridors of Saint-Martin, her habit bundled about her, thinking of Marcebru even as she did of Our Lord. These two loves were her joy and her burden. And the poem was his talisman against losing her. Outremer may have been his destination, but her deep pool of spirit was his home.

That evening I attended service in the chapel.

About a half a dozen nuns were there, though I noticed that the abbess was not present. The service was performed in Latin, a sign that Saint-Martin continued to observe the old rule.

Later I ate supper in the refectory with the nuns, a simple meal of boiled vegetables washed down with local wine. The frescoes on the walls, depicting the Last Supper, were painted in the austere Catalan style. Horace Winterton was here too, it seemed, arguing their primacy in the history of Western art. Certainly they evoked a rigor not visible in earlier styles.

After supper the guest mistress approached to ask me whether I was ready to meet the abbess. I inquired whether she might be ill, or tired, since I had not seen her in church or later at supper. Perhaps she would like to postpone our talk.

"Not at all," replied the guest mistress. "Because of infirmity, she has trouble leaving her rooms. This doesn't mean she is not with us in spirit."

"Abbess Stephanie is ill?"

"Age, monsieur, is a mountain pass over which she has no wish to stumble."

I followed the guest mistress to another part of the monastery. Eventually I was ushered into a bare reception room partitioned by a loosely barred window popular in enclosed monastic orders. Inside the far room I noticed a doorway.

"Wait here," the guest mistress advised. "I will bring the abbess."

Presently the door opened and Abbess Stephanie entered in a wheelchair. The guest mistress kissed the abbess's hand and retired, leaving us to stare at one another through the wooden bars. Together, it seemed, we were caged.

Before me was a woman whose frail limbs implied her considerable age. A pointed nose suggested a noble disposition. Her cheeks were soft, and her eyes did not waver. Gripping the armrests on the wheelchair, her hands looked like they had lost the power to make the sign of the cross but had gained something else. They were hands of acceptance, reconciliation, and trust. Abbess Stephanie's manner was that of a person who had gone beyond suffering and was now enjoying a kind of contentment denied to others.

"Monsieur, I believe you have come to inquire about Amedée de Jois," the abbess began.

Stunned, I was unwilling to accept that she took my mind and so knew my intentions.

"Spirits are abroad, monsieur. They know our thoughts. It is no accident that they announced your arrival. We welcome you in the name of all those good souls who have lived here in the past. Blessedness can be contagious if you allow the stones of Saint-Martin to breathe on you."

Briefly I outlined the reason for my journey to Saint-Martin, informing the abbess of all the people I had met on the road. I told her how these contacts had changed me, and how I wanted to know more about Amedée de Jois. Abbess Stephanie allowed me to complete my story before attempting to reply.

"The memory of Sister Amedée haunts us," she said.

"She must have been greatly loved."

"She was born into a noble family from Castres. A town of weavers, it is understandable that she would have come in contact with the Cathars in her youth. Her father, Count Jacques, we know to have been sympathetic to their cause."

"Yet she took her vows as a Catholic rather than follow her family into heresy."

"It is not so strange," replied Abbess Stephanie.

"How did she meet Marcebru?"

"We know nothing of their first encounter, except that they had met before Sister Amedée took the veil. Tradition tells us the poet appeared at the court of Castres after a time in Spain. Shortly thereafter, the poet declared Amedée de Jois to be his *fin' amors*. From then on his poetry began to reflect his undying love for her. It was not an ordinary love."

"Marcebru was no ordinary man," I said.

"Together, living their unique love, they finally

outgrew themselves. This is the essence of their lives. It is a story that goes beyond normal affection between people."

"Why, then, did she choose to take her own life?"

"'Give' and 'take' imply willful acts, monsieur. They also suggest our desire to make judgments. We do not know why Sister Amedée departed this world, or whether it was of her own volition. It may be that rather than take her own life, she was indeed taken."

"I don't think I follow you, your grace."

"When we adopt the veil our lives become bound by the Trinity, monsieur. One represents unity, the divine love of God. Two represents multiplicity, the things of this world. And three represents infinity, the possibility we share of knowing God's love. The Trinity oversees our suffering and our hope. When Sister Amedée's mute form was found at the foot of the ravine below the cloisters one morning in 1196, it was assumed by all that she had committed suicide. Otherwise, how did she get there? Word quickly spread throughout Languedoc that she had died by a secret act of *endura*."

"We do know she was found wearing a Cathar belt."

"The belt may have been a sign of old allegiances, a gift from her family that, for personal reasons, she did not have the courage to abandon. Who can say what her motives were for wearing it? All of us bear the burden of our past. Memory of a loss, a disappointment perhaps, we carry these throughout our lives, a belt of pain that strengthens us. It is not for me to say whether Sister Amedée was drawn into heresy, or whether she felt the need to maintain two beliefs."

"As a Cathar and Catholic, is this possible?"

"All things are possible, monsieur," replied Abbess Stephanie, her aging hands gripping the armrests on her wheelchair. "Speaking personally, and I feel that you will allow me that privilege, I have long since come to accept that there is no end to the ways we choose to believe. Your friend Marcebru made the poem his act of faith. He journeyed to world's end in pursuit of it. Did not Sister Amedée do the same? When I mentioned earlier how we who take the veil are bound by the mysterious nature of the Trinity, I failed to mention that in Sister Amedée's case she managed to transform the idea of infinity into excess."

"She died from loving too much?" I inquired.

"We nuns, monsieur, dedicate ourselves to the love of God. We do not seek to express love in any other way. Such a love can be dangerous, since it enjoins us to give up all contact with our bodies. In doing so, we distance ourselves from the love that occurs between a man and a woman. This is our choice, and our path. We do not regret it, but still . . ." Abbess Stephanie's voice trailed away.

"You are suggesting that Amedée de Jois was a victim of a double love? The love of God and that of Marcebru?"

"It is not impossible. Spirit and poet are not so different, after all. Perhaps she fell in love with the spirit in Marcebru. He was her *fin' amors*. All I ask of you, monsieur, is that you do not question Sister Amedée's death too closely. Refrain from analyzing it—how shall I say?—in the modern manner. I can tell you there were no marks found on her body. Her fall into the ravine had been more in the nature of a flight than a descent. She died of a love that was inexpressible. For a time, quite naturally, the poet tried to keep her alive with his words, bring her back to life. When these failed him, he must have felt his own demise was imminent."

"The poet never gives up the destiny of the word. It is his reason for being," I argued.

"I was talking of the word releasing itself from him. Freeing him from its oppression."

"Which, I assume, can only lead to the birth of a deep, unplumbable stillness."

"If it were a reliquary, I would press it to my lips," Abbess Stephanie admitted, her lips quivering with emotion.

Silence presided over us as we allowed the spirit of Amedée de Jois to enter the room. She was there, hovering above us, a pair of wings trembling like a hawk's before it plummets toward its prey. Her descent into the ravine had been the completion of a supreme act of release, while for Marcebru she had become the perfect poem, a line of verse whose meaning went beyond words. For me, too, she was now the embodiment of something new—a self-recognition and an understanding of my place in their drama.

This double love of Amedée de Jois, her infatuation with both poet and spirit, was the beginning of a revelation for me. Her death suggested a link between proximity and distance, between assuming and not-knowing, as if this was the only path to follow. I had arrived at a point where the sum of my life mattered little in contrast to a death that was both intimate, ever present, yet mysterious.

The guest mistress tiptoed into the room. Abbess Stephanie, meanwhile, had fallen asleep in her wheelchair. Reverie had become her pillow.

"Monsieur," the guest mistress whispered, "I trust that I have left enough blankets in your room."

"Cold is not my greatest concern," I said.

Dazed, I turned and walked toward the door. The corridor beyond was lit by a solitary globe.

———

25

THE BRIDGE
AT USSEL

—

I HAD REACHED THE END of the road.
Mount Canigou loomed. Go no further, it seemed to
say—the mystery surrounding Amedée de Jois must
remain as it is. A poet's silence and a woman's death
should not matter that much, anyway. But they did.
I had invested too much of myself in their lives not to
feel I had something to lose. In a sense, they had become a part of my own.

I could be forgiven for thinking this way. Gazing
at Mount Canigou that morning, its craggy slopes already flecked with early snow, I began to see that its
solitary grandeur was no different from life. I had
been too busy trying to justify Amedée de Jois's death
to see that it might have a meaning for those who
had known her. Abbess Stephanie seemed to think

so. She had allowed its mystery to remain as strong as it ever was.

In Amedée de Jois's case it may well have been so. Her nature had determined that she go beyond living. *She had found a reason for dying.* I never imagined that the reason for living might be to find some justification for death. Giving up her life had been an act of gratitude. Rather than die to be reborn in another body, as her Cathar heritage might suggest, she had chosen to release herself from this constant round of suffering and so become a gift to others.

No wonder Marcebru had fallen silent. Through her he had discovered his true voice. She was thunder to his lightning. She had absorbed his incandescence and made it a part of her own. His decision to abandon poetry at her death only accentuated his loss. Like a passing storm, his emotions were stripped of their power to reproach his age in the way he had always done in the past. Marcebru had become a living ghost, inhabiting her death with a silence of his own.

In spite of my earlier feelings of estrangement, my sympathy for the man remained the same. Time did not separate us, nor language, nor the rhythm of the poem. After all, we both wanted to render the world as a quality that eluded the net of our senses. The pursuit of *fin' amors* as a value capable of transforming our lives was common to both of us. Only now did I realize how deeply imbedded Marcebru had been in the physical world. Had he not gone to it in the hope of reconciling himself to his loss?

My conversation with Abbess Stephanie had reminded me that a person's motivations do not always lie on the surface of one's actions. What justifies a person's life is not always obvious. Those who live intensely often rely more on a painful gestation of consciousness than on any normal reasons for acting as they do. For them, thinking isn't enough. Their aim is to translate their life into something of lasting power, the very stuff of poetry.

"Let those white swans fly to your rescue," I heard Horace's voice addressing me in my thoughts. "Their perfection counts for more than the words of philosophers."

It was a voice demanding me to return to Ussel, to that place which marked the end of Marcebru's journey and the beginning of my own. Knowing what I knew now, it was time to return and so complete a full circle. It was, after all, the circle of knowledge.

My Deux Chevaux suddenly grew wings. It trundled along back roads, around hills, across bridges, over mountains, through sleepy villages, past ruined castles, and under chestnut trees. It followed streams, negotiated cobbled lanes, stopped at roundabouts, parked outside cafés, and cooled down in hotel courtyards. It paused at petrol stations, picked up hitchhikers, slowed at pedestrian crossings, waited while cows ambled across roads. And all the while it carried on the seat beside me an echo of the journey Marcebru had made, and of the one I had made retracing his footsteps.

Once more Aquitaine unraveled before me, a spool of memories. A sense of *déjà vu* was woven into every hour of the day. Cathar redoubts on hilltops, tympana on churches covered with religious carvings, barbicans filled with arrow slits, modillions on walls supporting urns blossoming with flowers, jacquemarts on clocktowers hammering out the hour, belfries without bells, foliated scrolls depicted as leaves on friezes, diagonal arches and frescoes, rood screens between nave and chancel in country churches, megaliths and dolmens on riverbends, caves and gorges and the stony silence of village squares—all these made the trip back to Ussel a nostalgic one for me. The land of Oc had become its own poem.

I felt a new sense of resolution while I drove, as if the journey had realized something important for me too. I had followed Marcebru's steps through Aquitaine in a bid to fathom his motives. The chance encounters with various people, and the places I visited, all offered me some key. It seemed his silence had become more imperious as long as the death roll continued to grow. The words of others had become a substitute for his own. Marcebru had sacrificed any attempt to shelter something from death in the act of writing.

At some point on his journey north the death roll must have become too great a weight. The burden of carrying its message across Aquitaine toward an unknown destination had finally proved too much. It probably dawned on him that not even the power of words could bring Amedée de Jois back. This must have galled him, knowing that her life was growing more distant than ever, a flickering lamp on a departing coach.

A cold wind was blowing when I reached Ussel late in the afternoon. A lip-whitening chill froze the air. People were already wearing overcoats. I entered the same hotel where I had stayed previously, hoping to find a room available. I was in luck: the receptionist recognized me at once and offered me my old room overlooking the river.

"There's a letter for you," she said.

"Who would know of my intention to return to Ussel?" I remarked, puzzled by this coincidence.

"A man wearing a rather extravagant bow tie delivered it by hand."

"R.! Who else but he anticipates my every move?"

I climbed the stairs to my room. Laying my travel items on the bed, I thumbed open the bulky envelope. Two letters were inside. R.'s unmistakable handwriting greeted my gaze first.

My Friend,

Such an extraordinary journey! Welcome home. The mystery surrounding Marcebru's death roll has proved to be as subtle as the arches supporting a groined vaulting. I envy you your patience. You have built a singular edifice, one that will withstand time I'm sure.

But enough! The death roll has been your boon companion. It has taken you into every nook and cranny of the medieval mind. Lucky man! I wish I might say that I knew the stonemasons of old in the way you seem to know Marcebru and his ilk.

The death roll is a pathway forged through the thicket of anguish. People simply do not know how to react to death, except to resort to pious condolences. These, as you know, are no match for the sheer omnipotence of the soul's flight. It revels in the distance it places between itself and existence.

What I wanted to tell you is this: the scholar who translated the death roll took a turn for the worse. His health declined rapidly after you left. It was almost as if, by handing over the death roll to you, he had granted you his life. He passed away a week ago, content with his span of years, whispering something about endura *as he lapsed into unconsciousness.*

But this was not before he asked me to present to you the enclosed letter. He requested me to pass it on, unopened, claiming that it contained the final passages of the death roll, which he had not yet translated when he gave it to you. His last words to me were: "Pass this on to your friend. Tell him they are the translation of certain pages I fear might change the world." He said that you would understand.

I commend these pages to you in his name. It is not often I have found myself a divine messenger of sorts. Let me assure you that the scholar believed they were pertinent to your inquiry.

In England, when you return, let us try to meet in the nave of Salisbury Cathedral. Its elegance, I'm sure, will generate thoughts worthy of the great height of its transept.

Once again, my friend, adieux.

I returned the letter to its envelope. The other note I laid on the desk unopened. I wondered why the elderly scholar would have withheld these pages until now. The knowledge that he was about to die may have instilled in him some urgency to complete his lifelong work and pass it on. If they were the final entries of the death roll, I hardly dared to read them. Instead I recalled the lines of the first poem I had read in the death roll all those weeks ago, written by Willemus. His words rose to my lips:

> Touch her hem, on it phrases are filigree.
> There is more to life than death.

Could any verse match the beauty of these lines as a measure of someone's admiration for another? Finally I plucked up the courage to open the second envelope. Reading it made me realize how the scholar had bequeathed to me a most trenchant eulogy celebrating one man's battle with his dream of creating a perfect poem:

> It is hard to live with silence
> Since real silence is death.
> I have journeyed to Palestine
> And to Spain, I, Marcebru,
> In search of a desert
> Able to contain who I am.
> Among perfidious stones
> Voices lurked, small scorpions
> Of delight eager to poison me
> With the sting of their words.
>
> Queen of my heart, grant me
> Unguents to heal this wound:

In love honorable, a sword
At the throat of delusion
Ready to defend Youth, child
Of this world and the next,
Champion of gestures
Which make me anonymous,
Yes, a well without water.

Drained of my purpose
You have made me complete;
The great poem I have worn
In all weather now hangs
In tatters from my shoulders.
I, Marcebru, stalk the high passes
Where bandits hide, ready
To steal from me old coins
Minted in the foundry of sense.

Death is its own sweet nectar,
And yours tastes of ripened fruit.
I stand by the bridge at Ussel
Recalling our love, nurtured
By distance and the knowledge
That past and future are joined.
Grant me remission from loneliness
And the cold hands of time
Clutching hard at my throat.

Take me, a scullion of life
In the pay of poetry, song,
And the glory of *fin' amors,*
Toward the summit of a
Mountain, from which one path
Leads and another returns.
I hold your hand, a pilgrim
On the road to a victory
More poignant than thought.

"A victory more poignant than thought," I kept
reading over and over again. This victory, I now realized, was the one I hoped to achieve over the futility
of expression. Marcebru, it seemed, had heard my
call. He had recognized in me the desire to go beyond language in my attempt to render the most difficult of all themes: that of the importance of
restraint as the principle and adjunct to speech.

Yet Marcebru had given me this: he, the *orpailleur* of language, the man who carried in his treasure chest those gems that go to make up the perfect
poem, the translator of Rosetta Stones, the bearer of
watermarks, the armorer of expression, the founder
of brotherhoods, the critic of false lovers, the painter
of ruins, the observer of fireballs, the concealer of
names, the carver of faceless images, the dreamer of

lizards, the white friend, court poet, songster, and keen observer of swans.

I felt his presence in the room, powerful yet remote. It was as if Marcebru had left the death roll in my care. Outside, the night had settled into its winter chill, the stream below streaked with light from the hotel windows. Between us Marcebru and I were wintering in memory, compatriots of the word. The death roll was our bond. Together we were joined by its pages and its fate.

I put on my coat. Collecting the death roll and Marcebru's last poem, I walked toward the door. There was nowhere to go but into the streets of Ussel. I turned the corner and made my way toward the bridge. The street lamps shone limpidly. Before me, the rising span of the bridge clung to each riverbank like hawsers of a ship that had recently berthed. How many generations of people had walked its decks, ignorant of what had occurred at this spot?

I leaned over the wall and gazed at the stream. It was as still as ice. I wondered then whether it had already frozen over. Suddenly I knew what Marcebru wanted, and why I had been drawn into this mystery. Of course! The death roll was a poem written by men and women in celebration of their own failures and limitations, their own victories and triumphs. These were its theme, the contribution to its singular and everlasting form. For some mysterious reason, too, I had been called upon to become its custodian, thus securing for them a place in the history of his loss.

Taking a deep breath, I reached out over the wall and flung the death roll into the river. Slowly it began to sink, a hulk in the final act of being scuttled. I watched it drift away from the bridge, turning as it went, fluttering, pirouetting in the current. It floated downstream, its pages unfolding, a blossom of words. The lights from the hotel above sparkled against what was already a half-submerged text. Finally it disappeared into the darkness.

━━

26

IN THE CATHEDRAL

—

Thus did I return to England and to my rendezvous with R. in the nave of Salisbury Cathedral, among the effigies of bishops and knights carved in splendid marble. To that meeting I also invited Horace Winterton, begging him to forsake his swans and the sleepy waters of the Thames.

"From what you have told us," Horace pronounced, "there is no end to this document that you threw away."

"I felt Marcebru had no wish to see his failure paraded before the world," I replied.

"Ah, that river of secrets," added R., arranging his bow tie. "Without it, where would we go to retrieve what we most desire?"

"You had no qualms?" Horace invited, conscious of the burden of responsibility on my shoulders.

"Come, come," R. interposed. "As risky as his gesture was, the death roll had already been consigned to the waters. All our friend has done, Horace, was symbolically recapitulate Marcebru's final act. But this time the document was being put to rest."

"It was an impulse on my part, no more," I defended.

"Let us say that you were merely acting in the best interests of the poet." Horace tried to alleviate my anxiety.

"Such a balm," R. chided.

They both had a point. It was as if the Rosetta Stone and Marcebru's death roll lay in repose in the same seductive chamber. Together they presided over meaning. All I had done was enter their solitude and sound a bell. Between them Marcebru and Amedée de Jois lay side by side, two effigies in their prime, their candor now mine.

"You realize the task in front of you," Horace remarked.

"How so?" R. demanded, gazing upward at his beloved vaulting, so calmly intricate.

"Our friend must somehow put to rest what we, each in our own way, have unwittingly unleashed," Horace added.

"By its nature perfection is a matter of extreme gravity, I agree," R. responded.

"For this reason, it seems, Amedée de Jois had no choice but to *descend*."

Horace's statement possessed all the hallmarks of his acute mind. Only he would have recognized that gravity and perfection were not opposed. Amedée de Jois had been weighed down by her desire to step beyond herself, and not even Marcebru's attempt to capture her in a poem could prevent her from falling.

"I know what my task is," I said.

"Ah, then tell us," R. took my arm in his as the four of us proceeded to walk around the narthex of the cathedral. Filets of light from the windows above mingled with our steps.

"Welcome to the Brotherhood," Horace added, reminding us all of M. de Langue's lonely vigil in Carcassonne.

"Let me say that I have been taken aback by my recent experience," I began. "Stalking a poet is no grouse hunt. His flightiness and cunning remind me of the behavior of certain animals that take delight in eluding the huntsman. I am thinking of pumas. Moreover, his allegiance to the 'closed style' in matters of expression reminds me of the platypus's burrow, whose opening lies below the surface of a pool. This curious creature only appears to us submerged."

"As Marcebru does, immersed in his poems," Horace said.

"I know now what he means to me," I continued. "His footsteps across Aquitaine partake of something immeasurable. He sought a remedy for his grief by asking all those whom he met to share with him their fate. In time, a new vision of the woman that he loved was revealed to him. Her nature became a carefully crafted object. Finally, the woman that he once knew disappeared under a scroll of words, and in her place there arose another person. It was more than he could take."

"He grew to resent her?" R. was incredulous.

"Marcebru began to realize that he had imprisoned her in language. She who was the victim also became his jailer. Her desire to end life both fascinated and repelled him. At first the meaning of this act eluded him—he, the prince of expression. Then he saw that by abandoning argument in favor of action, Amedée de Jois was only alerting him to what he lacked in himself."

"What on earth could that be?" Horace inquired, allowing his hand to touch a tomb effigy as we passed.

"His humanity," I said.

My friends stopped in their tracks. Without uttering a word they looked at me, then at each other. I could tell what they were thinking. Was I denouncing the object of my obsession? More importantly, was I betraying Marcebru at the moment when he needed me most?

"You mentioned your encounter with the Rosetta Stone," Horace remarked, hoping to change the subject and so smooth troubled waters.

"All these attempts to clarify what we mean," I argued, recalling Champollion's lifelong commitment to extinct languages, "they are what finally undid Marcebru. He longed to experience life with the same intensity that he expressed it. He did not want to see himself reduced to a few indecipherable inscriptions on a piece of basalt. No. He knew that if he must choose between language and life, then he had no alternative but to choose the latter."

"And so he threw the death roll into the river as a gesture of rebuke toward himself," R. observed.

"With all the finesse of a javelin," added Horace.

There, it was said. Marcebru had finally abandoned an impossible love in favor of life. His humanity depended on it. Whatever the Cathars had stood for, they did not stand for the ultimate exuberance to which he was drawn. Whatever Amedée de Jois had stood for, she could not stand for the power that drove him toward expressing himself. *Endura* was not the act of releasing the soul from the prison of the body so much as sanctioning a fear of life.

"I salute you, my friend," R. announced, releasing my arm. "Few of us manage to enter such a tragic age as you have done, and come out unscathed."

"Oh, but I am not," I replied.

Horace halted in his march toward the cathedral entrance. He turned.

"I take it you are not scarred or ill in any way," he said.

I shook my head. At the same time, I knew what I had to do: to renovate consciousness by way of a prolonged act of meditation and courage. I must approach the loom of life once more, as Marcebru had done before me, and weave on it a piece of cloth whose patterns reflected all the discordancy of our time. The heart, after all, must be provided with a new outlet in which necessity and freedom might intermingle. Only then would I do justice to the memory of Marcebru, and to his attempt to break Amedée de Jois's fall into anonymity.

"Recuperation does not depend upon whether we are ill or not," I said, as we quit the cathedral and walked out into soft sunlight.

━━━━━

eza que non tref fail· Et qene
fti amanoiz· Aiffi con feral
temps betbuz·

Avones quef auelf hom fep
lagn· Can uel temps elaf pa
uuz· Con ttal teprang· Quelz
auile met cuber gang· Cu nē
eftru qui non ef ueftiz· por
amar drma pailla uuz·
Queft em fenblan atu· Al fet
quan fon plen eqagut· Apref
lo tun· E non loz ne fouel ma
tn· Auz uutal fen tos acrupit·
Cant tun lons temps non fo
neuz·
ouenz bomes debel fenblan·